The
MANY
WORLDS
of
ALBIE
BRIGHT

The

MANY
WORLDS
of
ALBIE
BRIGHT

CHRISTOPHER EDGE

DELACORTE PRESS

Text copyright © 2016 by Christopher Edge
Jacket art and interior illustrations copyright © 2017 by Chuck Groenink

All rights reserved. Published in the United States by Delacorte Press, an imprint of Random House Children's Books, a division of Penguin Random House LLC, New York. Originally published in different form and in paperback by Nosy Crow, London, in 2016.

Delacorte Press is a registered trademark and the colophon is a trademark of Penguin Random House LLC.

Visit us on the Web! randomhousekids.com

Educators and librarians, for a variety of teaching tools, visit us at RHTeachersLibrarians.com

Library of Congress Cataloging-in-Publication Data is available upon request.
ISBN 978-1-5247-1357-7 (hardcover) — ISBN 978-1-5247-1359-1 (lib. bdg.)
ISBN 978-1-5247-1358-4 (ebook)

The text of this book is set in 12.25-point Goudy Old Style.
Interior design by Vikki Sheatsley

Printed in the United States of America
10 9 8 7 6 5 4 3 2 1
First American Edition

For Chrissie, Alex, and Josie
in every universe

"But do you really mean, Sir," said Peter, "that there could be other worlds—all over the place, just round the corner—like that?"

"Nothing is more probable," said the Professor, taking off his spectacles and beginning to polish them, while he muttered to himself, "I wonder what they *do* teach them at these schools."

—C. S. Lewis, *The Lion, the Witch and the Wardrobe*

IT WAS MY DAD WHO GAVE ME THE IDEA OF using quantum physics to find my mum.

She died two weeks ago. Her funeral was on Tuesday. It was at St. Thomas's Church in the village. At first Dad said he wanted something called a humanist funeral without any "religious mumbo jumbo," but Granddad Joe wasn't having this. "She's not a *humanist*," he'd said, almost spitting out his tea when Dad tried to explain. "She's my daughter."

He said that Mum had been christened at St. Thomas's Church when she was a baby, and he wanted her ashes buried there too, right next to Grandma Joyce, looking out toward the wind turbines and the mine at the edge of the moors.

That's where Mum used to work—down in the pit. She wasn't a coal miner; she was a *scientist*. You see, Clackthorpe Pit is one of the deepest mines in Great Britain, and when the coal ran out, it was scientists searching for the secrets of the universe who moved in there instead. Down at the bottom of the mine, they could use all their hightech equipment without any cosmic rays interfering with their experiments.

Cosmic rays are radiation from outer space. Every second of the day, dozens of these cosmic rays zip through your body and you don't even notice a thing. Don't worry, they won't turn you into a bug-eyed mutant, but they can seriously mess up the kind of experiments Mum and Dad do, so that's why they've got to hide them away underground.

Mum and Dad used to joke that their first date was a thousand meters beneath the moors. They went down into the mine looking for dark matter—the invisible glue that sticks the universe together—and found each other instead. They got married, and (skipping the embarrassing biology bit) eight months later I showed up. Albert Stephen Bright. I was named after Mum and Dad's favorite scientists, Albert Einstein and Stephen Hawking, but everyone calls me Albie for short.

According to my mum, my early arrival was a bit like the big bang—a complete surprise, and pretty scary too— and I ended up staying in the hospital until I was nearly four months old. Then, when I finally got better, Mum and Dad took me with them when they went to work at CERN in Switzerland.

CERN is like Disneyland for scientists. It's where the World Wide Web was invented, and now it's the home of the Large Hadron Collider. In case you haven't seen it on TV, the Large Hadron Collider is the biggest machine in the world. It's sixteen and a half miles long and weighs a whopping 38,000 tons. That's why it's called the *Large* Hadron Collider. Scientists built the LHC to look inside the smallest things in the universe: atoms.

Everything in the universe is made out of atoms— you, me, this piece of paper, even the sun. And the thing about atoms is they're small—very small. To give you an idea of how incredibly tiny I'm talking here, take a look at the period at the end of this sentence. Had a good look? Now, that period has eight trillion atoms inside it. That's 8,000,000,000,000 atoms. Count those zeroes. There are more atoms in that period than there are people alive in the world today. That's pretty amazing, don't you think? And every atom is made up of even smaller particles called protons, neutrons, and electrons.

When I asked Mum why she needed such a big machine to look inside something so small, she told me that the Large Hadron Collider is like an underground race-track for atoms, but the winner is the one who has the biggest crash. In the collider, these tiny particles race around and around in circles, getting faster and faster until they smash together at almost the speed of light. Mum said this creates a mini big bang—a bit like the one that made the universe—and by studying this, Mum and Dad hoped to find out exactly how everything began.

There was just one problem. In addition to those mini big bangs, it turned out that smashing atoms together at nearly the speed of light might make mini black holes too. A black hole is like an invisible vacuum cleaner in outer space, sucking up anything that gets too close. This book my dad wrote says that the gravity inside a black hole is so strong that not even light can escape. If you tried to fly a spaceship past for a closer look, you'd get sucked inside the black hole and turned into spaghetti.

Of course, the idea of the Large Hadron Collider creating a black hole here on Earth wasn't that popular. Before you knew it, TV news crews from around the world were turning up at CERN to accuse Mum, Dad, and the rest of the scientists there of plotting to DESTROY THE WORLD! It ended up being my dad who was pushed in front of the TV cameras to explain how this was totally ridiculous and that any black holes that *were* created inside the collider would evaporate instantly without Earth being sucked inside out.

That's when he got discovered by a talent scout. A TV company offered Dad the chance to make his own series,

Ben Bright's Guide to the Universe: Everything You Ever Wanted to Know About Space for People Who Hated Science at School. It turned out that quite a lot of people hated science at school, because eight million people ended up watching. One TV reviewer even nicknamed my dad The Man Who Can Explain Everything, but to be honest, he wasn't much help with my homework. Most of the time he wasn't even home, since he was flying around the world filming cool science stuff for his next TV show.

Whenever Dad did turn up to collect me from school, I usually ended up hanging around waiting while my teachers took a selfie with him. It was seriously embarrassing, but Mum didn't seem to mind. She used to joke that all the time Dad spent being a TV star just gave her more time to get on with the real science, and that she'd win a Nobel Prize before him.

That was before Mum got the news that changed everything.

She'd gone for one of the health checks given to all the scientists at the LHC, and a shadow had shown up on one of the scans. Cancer. And with that one word, Mum and Dad packed up everything and we came back to Great Britain and the NHS.

We moved back into our old house in Clackthorpe, and I watched Dad ferry Mum to the hospital and back again, trying treatment after treatment until the doctors finally said there was no point in trying anything else. I watched Mum lose her hair, her smile, and finally all hope. There was just enough time for me to get angry, and then she was gone, leaving a supermassive black hole behind.

That's how I ended up standing at the front of St. Thomas's Church, staring at her coffin. The church was filled with Mum and Dad's family and friends: Granddad Joe, Aunt Sophie and the twins, scientists from the Large Hadron Collider and from the mine at the edge of the village. There were people from TV and Mum's old school friends. Everyone had come to say goodbye.

When the vicar started to speak, Dad grabbed hold of my hand and held on to it tightly. It was almost like he wanted to make sure I didn't disappear on him too, but it just made me feel like a little kid. Granddad Joe was holding on to my other hand, and I had to sit there between them, just wishing I could stick my fingers in my ears. I didn't want to hear any of it, but I can remember every word.

"Today we come together to remember Charlotte Elizabeth Bright, taken from this world at the age of thirty-nine, leaving behind her husband, Ben, and her son, Albie. Charlotte was not only a devoted wife, loving mother, and beloved daughter, but also a scientist of world renown. With her work at the Large Hadron Collider, Charlotte shined a light into the unexplored corners of the cosmos, helping us all understand a little more about the wonder of creation. Atoms and stars, the speed of light, and the beat of the human heart—all of these come from a power far greater than any machine ever built by the hand of man.

"And now Charlotte is in a place where such wonders will seem commonplace. A place of infinite beauty and splendor, where there is no sickness or pain, no sorrow or despair, only joy everlasting. I speak, of course, of heaven, where Charlotte will find the answers to every question she has ever asked about God's creation."

I wanted to put my hand up to ask the vicar my own question, but Dad and Granddad Joe wouldn't let go, so I just had to sit there and listen to him drone on. It was only after the funeral, when everyone else had gone home and Granddad Joe was snoring in his armchair, that I finally got the chance to ask Dad the question that was bugging me.

"How does the vicar *know* that Mum's in heaven?"

Sitting on the sofa, Dad blinked in surprise. As I waited for an answer, he opened and closed his mouth a few times, but no words actually came out.

"I mean, do *you* believe in heaven?" I asked him.

And that's when Dad started to tell me about quantum physics.

"Atoms and particles can behave in rather strange ways," he began. "There's a famous experiment called the double-slit experiment where scientists fire a single atom at two tiny holes in a wall." Grabbing hold of a piece of paper and a pen, Dad began to sketch out a diagram to explain.

"Now, sometimes in this experiment the atom goes through the left-hand hole, and sometimes it goes through the right-hand hole, but when nobody is looking, the atom appears to go through both holes at the same time."

Typical. I ask my dad a simple question and he tries to turn it into an episode of his TV show.

"Different scientists have come up with different theories about how the same atom can be in two places at once," Dad continued. "But some quantum physicists think that this is evidence of a parallel universe. They say that this universe—the world we live in—is just one of an infinite number of other universes. Every time our world is confronted with a choice—for example, whether the atom goes through the left-hand hole or the right-hand hole—it splits into new parallel worlds where each possibility actually happens."

"What do you mean 'new parallel worlds'?" I asked, still struggling to understand exactly why Dad was telling me this.

"Imagine a line of planet Earths all stretching into space," he said, "one after another like the line for the school bus. Every one of these parallel worlds is just like our planet, but with one tiny difference. In one of these parallel worlds you've just won the lottery, but in another world you've been eaten by a shark instead. Everything that can happen *does* happen somewhere."

Dad pulled that serious-looking face he does on TV whenever he's explaining a really tricky bit of science.

"Just think about it, Albie. If this is true for a single atom when it goes through both holes in the wall, then it's true for you and me too. We're all made out of atoms. Your mum's cancer was caused by a single cell in her body going rogue, but according to quantum physics there's a parallel universe where this never happened—your mum never got cancer and she's still alive and with us today." He tried to force his face into a smile. "That's a good thing to think, isn't it?"

My head spun as the full meaning of what Dad was telling me slowly sank in.

I'd asked Mum once why she had wanted to become a scientist. She'd told me that what she liked best about science was that it didn't just accept the way things are. Scientists ask questions, make discoveries, and sometimes end up changing the world. You only find out what is possible, she said, by trying to do the impossible.

If quantum physics said that my mum was still alive in some parallel universe, then maybe quantum physics could help me find her.

BUT BEFORE I COULD FIND OUT MORE ABOUT quantum physics, I had to go back to school.

You'd think that going to your mum's funeral on Tuesday would get you the rest of the week off, but not according to my dad.

"We need to get things back to normal," he says when I try to protest. "That's what Mum wanted, and that's what I'm going to make sure happens. That's why I'm going back to work at the Deep Mine Lab to check on my experiments, and you need to keep up on all your lessons."

"But I want to ask you about quantum—"

"We can talk tonight," he says firmly. "I've got to go now, Albie. Be good for Granddad and don't be late for school."

Same old excuses. Same old Dad. Always more interested in his work than he is in me. If Mum were here, she'd help me find out what I need to know about quantum physics. Which is kind of ironic if you think about it.

I could ask my mum anything. Why does the cheese on toast always go stringy? Where did all the dinosaurs go? How come people have two nostrils but only one mouth? Whatever question I asked her, she wouldn't just give me the right answer straightaway. Instead she'd usually ask me what I thought, and then we'd investigate it together. We'd make toasted cheese sandwiches, go looking for fossils, or even practice shooting out snot rockets until we worked out the answer for ourselves.

Now I'm left with The Man Who Can Explain Everything but Who Doesn't Have Any Time to Talk to Me.

So while Dad heads off underground, I show up late for school, only to find that my classroom has been turned into some mad scientist's laboratory. Every desk seems to be covered with cardboard tubes, helium balloons, and plastic bottles dripping with gloop. On the nearest table, Victoria Barnes is building a mountain out of mashed potato, while behind her Kiran Ahmed is fixing a parachute to a Buzz Lightyear action figure. Everybody is talking at once, the volume fast approaching the critical level that will send Miss Benjamin into meltdown.

Miss Benjamin is an NQT. This means she's not quite a teacher. On the plus side, this means we get to do fun stuff like this science fair she's set up, where everyone has to think up their own amazing experiment. Miss Benjamin even invited my dad to come along and judge the experiments next week, but he's already said he'll probably be too busy with his work at the lab.

But unlike a proper teacher, Miss Benjamin is rubbish at controlling us. The boiling point of water is 100 degrees Celsius. The boiling point of Miss Benjamin is 100 decibels. This is as loud as a motorcycle revving its engine or a jumbo jet taking off, and according to Miss Benjamin, it's the noise Class Six makes when we get "a little bit overexcited." Wesley MacNamara says she's like a volcano. When her left eye starts to twitch, that's when you know she's going to blow.

For the moment, Miss Benjamin has her left eye under control as she sits me down next to her desk.

"I'm so glad to see you back in class, Albie," she says. "We've all missed you while you've been away, and I think you're very brave to come back to school so soon."

I don't tell her that my dad has practically forced me to come back to school. Instead I just stare down at my shoes. Dad polished them before the funeral, but it looks more like he's painted them with dark matter instead. I've never seen them looking so black and shiny. Maybe if I keep staring at them for long enough, a black hole will swallow me up and get me out of this place.

"Now, I'm sure you're going to be fine," Miss Benjamin bores on, "but if you feel you need to take some time out of class, I've asked Mrs. Forest to keep a quiet corner for you in the library. If anything ever gets too much or you just want to be alone with your thoughts, all you need to do is tell me and you can go there right away. No questions asked."

At the back of the class, a helium balloon pops with a sudden bang. I look up at Miss Benjamin to check whether her left eye has started to twitch.

"I just want to get on with my work, miss."

"Of course," she replies with the faintest flutter of her eyelid. "Well, as you can hear, everyone is busy working on getting their experiments ready for the science fair next week, but you've still got time to start on your own project, Albie. Why don't you take a look at what Victoria and some of the others are doing? It might give you some ideas."

So while I head off to see why Victoria Barnes is making a mountain out of mashed potato, Miss Benjamin rushes to the back of the class to stop Wesley MacNamara from re-creating the big bang with the help of his compass.

Victoria Barnes is the most popular girl in our school. I know this because that's what she told me when I started at Clackthorpe Primary six months ago. "I'm the most popular girl in school. Your dad is on TV. We should be friends." Our "friendship" lasted until first period, when Victoria realized that Dad didn't have any celebrity friends on speed dial and I told her that the only way she'd get on his TV show was if he could film her falling into a supernova.

A supernova is a supergiant star that explodes in space. Imagine the biggest firework display you've ever seen and then multiply it by a trillion. That's what a supernova looks like. I didn't mean to annoy Victoria by saying this. I just got a bit mixed up when she said she wanted to be a big star on TV.

I watch as Victoria plasters another layer of slop over the slopes of her mountain. Her long blond hair is tied back in a ponytail, and the tip of her tongue is sticking out from the corner of her mouth as she concentrates.

"Why are you making a mountain out of mashed potato?" I ask her.

She looks up at me with a scowl.

"It's not mashed potato, lamebrain. It's papier-mâché." She plasters on the last of the gloopy mixture around a large round hole at the top of the mountain. "This is Mount Vesuvius."

Victoria knows my name is Albie, but by the end of my first day at school, she'd convinced most of Class 6 that it was really L.B. and told them they had to guess what the initials stood for. Lamebrain was her favorite suggestion, and she's made sure that it's stuck. I just ignore it now. Like Mum always told me, there are much worse things than someone calling you names.

Victoria takes a step back to inspect her creation. I can see now that what I thought was a mountain of mashed potato is actually strips of plain paper smothered in glue and molded into a peak. At the bottom of the slope, there's a row of Lego houses guarded by Lego Roman soldiers and plastic farm animals. Victoria points her brush at this Lego brick town.

"This is Pompeii. I borrowed the Lego soldiers from my little brother's bedroom, and the toy cows and sheep come from Earlyears. Miss Benjamin says it's one of the best science projects she's ever seen. Your dad had better choose me as the winner next week."

I don't want to set Victoria off again, so I decide not to mention that Dad probably won't be judging the science fair after all. Instead I ask why her mountain has a hole in it.

"It's not a mountain, lamebrain. It's a volcano. Mount Vesuvius erupted nearly two thousand years ago. When it blew its top, it buried the town of Pompeii under a layer of volcanic rocks and ash. Nobody could escape the deadly lava flow, and thousands of people were buried alive or burnt to a crisp." Victoria's eyes glitter as she describes the destruction. "And when I pour vinegar and baking soda into the crater of *my* volcano, then—KABLOOM! It's fireworks time."

I look down at one of the toy soldiers, his tiny spear pointing toward a plastic cow twice his size. I imagine Victoria's volcano burying his house under a tidal wave of bubbling lava.

"Why didn't the people try to escape?"

"Nobody knew that Vesuvius was going to erupt," Victoria replies smugly. "One minute they were sitting in the sun eating pizza, the next—KABLOOM! Total wipeout."

Mum used to tell me that I worry about things too much. Global warming, asteroids hitting Earth, whether her experiments would create a black hole that would destroy the known universe. If I'd lived in Pompeii, you wouldn't have caught me hanging around eating a hot and spicy pizza.

"Miss Benjamin told us about your mum," Victoria says. "She said we had to be extra nice to you when you came back to school."

Victoria's definition of being "extra nice" obviously doesn't include not calling me lamebrain, but it's what she says next that gives me a surprise.

"So do you want to come to my birthday party on Friday? It starts at seven o'clock in the village hall. There's going to be a DJ, a photo booth, a dance competition—I'm *so* going to win that—and tons of cool people. And my mum said I should invite you too, to cheer you up."

On a scale of completely miserable to totally cheered up, the thought of going to Victoria's birthday party scores pretty low. I don't like having my picture taken, and I can't dance to save my life. But Dad said we had to start getting things back to normal, so maybe I should give Victoria a second chance.

"Thanks," I tell her. "I'll ask my dad if I can come."

Victoria picks up another soldier and turns back toward her volcano. "Don't forget to bring me a present," she calls out over her shoulder.

"Did Victoria Barnes just invite you to her birthday party?" I hear Kiran whistle in surprise from the desk behind me. "Wow, I've seen everything now."

Kiran Ahmed is my best friend in Class 6. In fact, he's probably my only friend in Class 6. It's tricky trying to make friends when you start a new school in the middle of Year 6. Everyone else has known each other for the past six and a half years—they've learned their times tables and played football on the playground together, and they all remember when Wesley MacNamara carried out the Great Stick Insect Massacre in Year 2. Everyone's got all the friends they need, and nobody was going to waste any time making me feel welcome. Apart from Kiran, that is.

At first I thought he only wanted to be my friend because my dad was on TV—just like Victoria—but then I found out that Kiran is obsessed with space. He says he's going to be the first man to set foot on Mars, but if he can't make it that far, he'll settle for being the first British Asian astronaut instead. He's taking scuba-diving lessons at the swimming pool to practice being weightless, and he knows the name of every moon in the solar system.

"Check it out," he says, dangling Buzz Lightyear from

his mini parachute. "I'm sending this bad boy to infinity and beyond!"

Tied to the corner of Kiran's desk is a helium balloon in the shape of a My Little Pony. The end of the string holding it down is looped around Buzz Lightyear's utility belt.

"With a My Little Pony balloon?"

Kiran shakes his head. "I've got more than just one balloon. My dad bought a bunch off eBay—only nine ninety-nine plus postage and packing for a hundred balloons. He got them for my little sister's birthday party, but she's into Spider-Man now, so he gave them to me instead. Miss Benjamin is storing the rest in the stock cupboard until the day of the science fair. You've seen that film *Up*? Well, I'm going to use these helium balloons to send Buzz Lightyear into space. The first action figure to make it into orbit."

If Kiran can put Buzz Lightyear into space powered only by a flock of My Little Pony balloons, he's bound to win first prize at the science fair. There's just one problem with his plan to launch the first action-figure astronaut.

"The space shuttle *Discovery* took a Buzz Lightyear into orbit back in 2008," I tell him. "My dad showed a video of the toy Buzz floating around on the International Space Station when he did a countdown of the top five weirdest astronauts on his TV show. Buzz came in third behind a jellyfish and a Russian space dog called Laika."

Unfortunately, Kiran doesn't take this news very well. He bangs his Buzz Lightyear down on the desk, and Buzz's flight wings snap open as his voice box squawks, "To infinity . . . and beyond!"

"Not if you've already been there before," Kiran snaps at Buzz. "I want to be the first. There's got to be something special I can send into space. Something that's never been done before."

"How about a Lego spaceman?" I suggest, glancing back at Victoria's volcano. Maybe Kiran's balloons can airlift the Lego people of Pompeii to safety before Mount Vesuvius blows its top.

Kiran shakes his head.

"Nah, two Canadian kids sent a Lego man into space back in 2012. I saw their video on YouTube. That's what gave me the idea for the balloons." He starts to unhook the string from Buzz's utility belt. "Are you doing a project for the science fair? You can always help me out with mine if you haven't got time to do your own. You know—because of your mum."

The only science I'm interested in at the moment is quantum physics. But before I can explain this to Kiran, a loud shriek comes from the back of the classroom.

"Miss!" Lucy Webster shouts out. "Wesley let Mr. Sniffles out of his cage!"

Mr. Sniffles is the class hamster. Squeals and shouts follow his escape route across the desks, a furry brown streak weaving between test tubes and pots of Play-Doh as Miss Benjamin battles to make herself heard.

"Quiet! QUIET! *QUIET!*"

Snatching up Mr. Sniffles before he launches himself through an open window, Miss Benjamin turns to look at us. Her face is a volcanic shade of red and her left eye is twitching into overdrive.

"Class Six, this behavior is completely unacceptable! I will not allow such chaos in my room! If you can't work on your science fair experiments without disturbing the rest of the school, then you'll have to do a science test in silence instead."

Everybody groans.

"Quiet!" Miss Benjamin shouts again. Striding to the back of the classroom, she puts Mr. Sniffles safely back into his cage.

"I didn't mean to let him out, miss." Wesley MacNa-mara holds up a plastic tray filled with tiny green leaves. "I just thought he might like a nibble of my cress."

Miss Benjamin ignores Wesley, her left eye still twitching out an SOS.

"Now, everyone, pack away your experiments and get your pens and pencils out instead. Quiet! I don't want to hear another sound out of any of you until the bell rings for break time."

Brilliant. My first day back at school and I've got to take a science test. And unless all the questions are about quantum physics, this isn't going to help me find my mum.

Then I remember that Miss Benjamin has already given

me the excuse I need to get out of this test. While the rest of the class grumbles as they pack up their experiments, I put my hand up.

"Miss, can I take some time out, please? I'd like to go to the library."

"YOU'RE LOOKING FOR A BOOK ABOUT WHAT?"

Mrs. Forest peers at me over her glasses, her library stamp hovering over a pile of Horrible Histories.

"Quantum physics, miss. It's for my science project."

Mrs. Forest doesn't like to call herself a librarian. She says she's a book doctor who can prescribe the right book to anybody. The last book she gave me was called *Danny the Champion of the World,* and it was all about this boy called Danny who lives in an RV with his dad. His dad spends most of his time inventing all kinds of cool things like kites, go-karts, and fire balloons to make up for Danny's mum being dead. To be honest, I stopped reading it after a few chapters because it just reminded me how rubbish my own dad is. Everyone thinks it's really cool to have a TV-star dad who knows how the universe works, but I'd swap him any day for an ordinary dad who knows how to fly a kite.

In our last library lesson, Mrs. Forest told Class 6 she had books that could take us anywhere. Brand-new countries, unforgettable places, fantastic lands. That was when Wesley MacNamara put his hand up to tell her she was getting books mixed up with Ryanair. Everyone else laughed, but right now I just hope she can find me a book that will take me to a parallel universe.

Mrs. Forest puts her book stamper down and leads me to the nonfiction section, hidden away around the corner. Peering at the middle shelf, she frowns as she flicks through a row of books with blue stickers on their spines.

"All the science books are here, Albie, but I don't think you'll find any books about quantum physics. It's not on the key stage two curriculum, you see. Couldn't you ask your dad instead? He probably knows more about science than all the authors I've got here put together."

"He's too busy with his work," I quickly reply. "I just want a book to help me with the basics."

"Aha." Mrs. Forest pulls a book from the middle of the shelf. "It looks like your dad might be able to help after all."

As she hands me the book, I look down to see my dad's face staring back at me from the cover. *Ben Bright's Guide to the Universe: From Asteroids to X-ray Stars and Everything in Between.* After his TV series was such a big hit, Dad was asked to write this tie-in book for kids, and he locked himself away in his office to get it finished. It was the last summer we'd had together as a family before everything went wrong, and he'd just wasted it.

At the time Mum had tried to make me feel better.

"He wants you to be proud of him, Albie. He's writing this book for you."

I didn't believe her then, but now I hope she was right.

Sitting down in the reading corner, I turn straightaway to the index. Asteroids, atoms, the big bang, black holes, cone radiation, dark matter, Einstein, and loads more words that I don't even understand. But halfway down the page, I find the entry I'm looking for: *Quantum physics: 108–109*.

I flip back to page 108, and this is the first thing I read:

If you think you understand quantum physics, then you don't understand quantum physics.

Great way to start an explanation, Dad.

Quantum physics is seriously weird science. It tries to explain the strange ways that atoms and particles behave. You see, inside the teeny-tiny quantum world, an atom or particle can be in more than one place at the same time and even be in two different states at once! According to quantum physics, everything is possible until you take a look.

I scratch my head. Dad has lost me already. How can something be in two different places or even be two different things at exactly the same time? It doesn't make any sense.

To give my brain a break, I take a look instead at the cartoon in the middle of the page. This shows what looks like a zombie cat trapped inside a box with a hammer hanging above a bottle of poison, a Geiger counter, and a glowing radioactive lump. The text underneath starts to explain this creepy image.

To show the strange effects of quantum physics, a scientist called Erwin Schrödinger invented an experiment. A cat is put inside a box with a lump of radioactive uranium that has a 50 percent chance of decaying. This means that at any moment, there is a 50 percent chance of a radioactive particle being emitted. If the Geiger counter detects a radioactive particle, it will trigger the hammer and smash open the bottle of poison. This will kill the cat. However, quantum physics says that until the box is opened and we take a look, the particle will be in both possible states—decayed and undecayed— simultaneously. This means the cat inside the box is dead and alive at the same time!

I shake my head as I try to make sense of this crazy experiment by the worst pet owner ever. How can a cat be dead and alive at exactly the same time? But before I can read the rest of the explanation, Wesley MacNamara whips the book out of my hands, crash landing next to me on the sofa.

"All right, lamebrain." He looks down at the cartoon in Dad's book. "Is this what you want to do for your science project? There's no way Miss Benjamin will let you create a radioactive zombie cat. She wouldn't even let me dissect a duck-billed platypus." Wesley's left eye starts to twitch in an exaggerated wink as he does his best Miss Benjamin impression. "*'They're a protected species, Wesley, and I will not have you cutting up cuddly Australian creatures in my classroom.'*"

Wesley growls, "They're furry freaks is what they are. Flippers like an otter, tail like a beaver, and an electricity-detecting beak like a mutant duck. I reckon they're actually weird-looking aliens who have come to invade our planet. That's why she doesn't want me chopping one up, in case I find out the truth."

This isn't actually the craziest thing I've ever heard Wesley say. When I started at Clackthorpe Primary, he told me that all the teachers there were shape-shifting extra-terrestrial reptiles who drank the blood of pupils to stay alive. When Miss Benjamin overheard this, she told Wesley that if she were a shape-shifting extraterrestrial reptile, she definitely wouldn't be working as an NQT. Then she said that if she heard him say that again, he'd be spending the rest of the week in detention. Wesley kept pretty quiet about bloodsucking alien teachers after that.

"What are you doing for your science project, then?" I ask him, trying to change the subject.

Wesley scowls. "She's got me growing cress in a cupboard—again. It's the same project I've done since Year One. But this time I've got a plan." He leans forward with a dangerous gleam in his eye. "When we go on our science trip tomorrow, I'm going to find out the truth about the duck-billed platypus, and you're going to help me."

I don't like the sound of this. Tomorrow Miss Benjamin is taking Class 6 on a school trip to the Clackthorpe Museum of Natural History and Mechanical Wonders. According to Kiran, this is the same school trip the class has been on for the past five years. He says it's called a museum but that it's really just a big house filled with loads of old junk. It used to belong to a Victorian explorer called Montague Wilkes, who left Clackthorpe to explore the world and sent everything he found back home before he died in the middle of Australia. I've had a look at the museum's website, and most of the things he found seem to be stuffed animals. I even spotted what looked like a duck-billed platypus stuck in a glass jar, and I now had the horrible feeling that this was part of Wesley's plan.

"Er, I don't think I'm going to be able to make it to the museum tomorrow. It was my mum's funeral yesterday—"

Nearly as fast as an atom whizzing around the Large

Hadron Collider, Wesley's fist shoots out to give me a dead arm.

"Ow!"

"You'd better help me tomorrow," Wesley warns me, "or else. And don't think you can use your mum as an excuse. Loads of people haven't got a mum, but you won't catch me crying about it."

Wesley lives with his nan and granddad. Kiran told me that Wesley's mum went on holiday to the Costa del Sol when Wesley was in Year 3 and never came back, but at least he gets to see her during the summer holidays.

Mrs. Forest suddenly appears like a library ninja from behind the geography and history bookshelves.

"What's going on here?" she says, a look of suspicion on her face. "Wesley, what are you doing out of class?"

"Miss Benjamin just sent me to check that Albie was OK, miss." Wesley drops my dad's book back into my lap as he gets up from the sofa. "You know, because of his mum and everything."

"And are you OK, Albie?" Mrs. Forest asks, looking down at the open book in my hands. "Did you find what you were looking for?"

As my dead arm aches, I look down again at the cartoon cat—the zombie pet still half alive and half dead. I don't have a clue how Schrödinger's crazy experiment could help me find my mum again. Quantum physics is seriously confusing. I need time to think, but there's no chance of that happening in school. Especially not with Wesley MacNamara dead-arming me to take part in his latest crazy scheme. I can feel my brain shutting down to take the pain away, leaving me empty inside. I've got to get out of here.

"I'm not sure, miss." I sniff, wiping a bit of wetness from the corner of my eye. "I just want to go home."

As Mrs. Forest bustles me off to the school office to phone Granddad Joe, Wesley calls out after me.

"See you tomorrow." I look back to see Wesley clench his fingers into a fist. "Or else," he mouths.

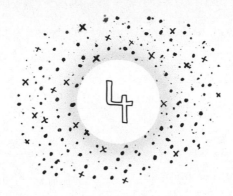

AFTER GRANDDAD JOE BRINGS ME HOME FROM
school, he sits me down in the kitchen to eat some lunch.

"You need to keep your strength up, Albie lad." Granddad scrapes what looks like a fried insole off the bottom of
the saucepan and slides it onto my plate. "This will soon
have you feeling right as rain."

I stare down at the plate in front of me. It looks like a
CSI crime scene in a burnt-out butcher's shop. I'd watched
Granddad Joe get sausages, streaky bacon, and black pud-
ding out of the fridge, but apart from a greasy lake of baked
beans, everything else on my plate has been burnt beyond
recognition. I give what looks like a roasted finger an ex-
perimental poke with my fork. Its prongs bounce straight

back, unable to pierce the banger's jet-black skin—now more nonstick saucepan than sausage.

Burnt food is carcinogenic. This means it can cause cancer. If I eat this sausage, then one cell in my body might mutate, and then another and another, and I wouldn't know that I had cancer until it was too late. Just like my mum.

I push the plate away. It isn't worth the risk.

"Come on, Albie. Eat up, lad."

I can hear the worry in Granddad Joe's voice, but this doesn't stop me from shaking my head.

"Mum usually makes me a sandwich," I tell him.

Granddad Joe sighs as he sinks down in the kitchen chair next to mine.

"Flaming hip," he mutters, wincing as he tries to bend his leg under the table. "I'm sorry, Albie. I can make you a sandwich if you want; just give me a minute."

Now he's got me feeling guilty, so I quickly shake my head again.

"It's OK, Granddad. I'll just eat my baked beans. It'll be a nice change."

Granddad Joe sighs again.

"There's been too much change around here lately, and none of it for the better."

After Mum died, the vicar came around to our house to talk about the funeral. As usual, Dad and Granddad

Joe ended up arguing about everything—the flowers, the hymns, the music. Dad wanted "Across the Universe" by the Beatles, but Granddad Joe said it wouldn't be a proper funeral unless you had "All Things Bright and Beautiful." In the end the vicar said that they would start the service with "All Things Bright and Beautiful" and then play "Across the Universe" at the end. I didn't care—the only song that made me think of Mum was the one we used to dance around the kitchen to, and I didn't want to hear that at the funeral. It'd only remind me that she wasn't here anymore.

Before he left, the vicar tried to give me a little booklet with a sad-looking rabbit on the front called *When Bunny Lost Her Mummy*. I told him I was too old for picture books, so he gave me the leaflet for grown-ups instead. This was called *Coping with Grief* and was all about the feelings you have when someone close to you dies. The leaflet said that most people go through five stages of grief.

1. DENIAL. This is the stage Dad's still stuck in. Disappearing down into the Deep Mine Lab and pretending that everything's OK. It's not, and I just wish he'd help me solve the problem instead of pretending that it doesn't exist.

2. ANGER. This is the stage Granddad Joe's in—that's why he keeps on arguing with my dad. Yesterday I overheard him telling Dad that it must have been working at the Large Hadron Collider that made Mum ill.

He said all that messing about with atoms must have given her cancer. Dad told him he was being ridiculous, but Granddad Joe just swore at him. I've never heard Granddad Joe swear before, so this shows you how angry he is.

3. BARGAINING. This is what I did when Mum first told me she had cancer. If I didn't step on a crack when I walked to school, then she'd be OK. If I saw a shooting star, then her cancer would go away. I'd drive myself crazy trying to make these challenges come true, but nothing ever worked.

4. DEPRESSION. This is how everyone at school thinks I should be feeling, but I haven't cried since Mum died. You see, I've realized that feeling sad is just a waste of time, and I've got to keep my focus on putting things right.

5. ACCEPTANCE. The leaflet said this final stage means facing the fact that the person who died is never coming back. But the thing is, since Dad told me there's a parallel universe where Mum's still alive, the only thing I've been able to think about is how I can get to see her again.

After taking a mouthful of beans, I push my plate away with a grimace. Granddad Joe might have scorched the sausages and bacon, but he's forgotten to heat up the baked beans.

"I'm not feeling very hungry at the moment."

"Let me make you a sandwich instead." Granddad Joe glances up at the clock on the kitchen wall. "There's a good film starting on the TV in a bit—*Back to the Future*. That used to be one of your mum's favorites. We could watch it together."

Whenever Dad was away for the weekend filming his TV show, Mum and I used to have movie marathons on a Saturday night. We'd binge-watch all the Star Wars films, Doctor Who box sets, and Back to the Future films. Mum said that *Back to the Future* was the film that made her want to become a scientist, but she was a bit disappointed that she hadn't managed to invent a time machine yet.

At the time I laughed, but now I remember what Granddad Joe said yesterday. Maybe if Mum hadn't become a scientist, she'd still be here today.

"Do you really think it was Mum's work that made her ill?"

Now it's Granddad Joe's turn to look guilty.

"I'm sorry, Albie," he says, taking off his glasses and rubbing his eyes. "I didn't mean for you to hear that." He sighs again, the last of his energy seeming to sag out of him in a single breath. "No, I don't think it made her ill. I was just looking for somebody to blame. I was as proud as punch of your mum when she told me she was going to be a scientist. The first in this family ever to go to university, and Cambridge University at that. Of course, I didn't understand any of that par-tic-u-lar physics stuff she was studying—atoms, protons, and all those thingamajigs—but after your Grandma Joyce died, she tried to explain it to me. We had the telescope out in the back garden, looking at the stars—just like we used to when your mum was a little girl. But this time she was telling me how everything we could see—all the thousands of stars in the sky—once fit into a tiny bubble a thousand times smaller than the head of a pin. She said that the big bang had created all this and her experiments were exploring how the universe was made. It sounded incredible to me, but, like I said to your mum, it needed someone to make the bang in the first place."

"So do *you* think Mum's in heaven, Granddad?"

"Of course she is," he replies confidently, pushing his glasses back into place. "Your grandma will be sorting her out with her wings as we speak." He gets up out of his chair with a wince. "So, shall I get the popcorn out?"

I shake my head. Watching *Back to the Future* again isn't going to help me find Mum.

"I think I'll skip the film, Granddad. I've got homework to do."

MY BEDROOM IS AT THE TOP OF THE HOUSE.
It's where all my stuff is. Actually, it's where most of Mum
and Dad's stuff is too. When we moved back to England,
there wasn't time to unpack everything with Dad taking
Mum to all her appointments at the hospital, and loads of
boxes filled with their work stuff got shoved out of the way
up in my room.

"It's just a temporary storage solution," Dad said when I
complained that I didn't have enough room to swing a cat.
"We'll sort them all out when your mum's feeling better."

So one half of my bedroom floor is still covered in cardboard boxes that I have to climb over every morning when
I get up. My bedroom back in Geneva was twice the size

of this attic room, and I had it just how I wanted it. There was a floor-to-ceiling bookcase for all my books and comics, a huge desk where I could set up my school projects, and a giant star map above my bed showing every constellation in the Milky Way.

I sit down on the edge of my bed. Now I've got no bookcase and piles of books and comics everywhere, a teeny desk that isn't big enough to do my homework on, and no room on the walls for my star map. The only poster I have put up is a map of the solar system, but this is just to disguise the rubbish decorating job Granddad Joe did when he heard we were moving back. This room used to be my nursery when I was a baby, and underneath his rushed paint job, you can still see the old Paddington Bear wallpaper if you squint.

In the middle of my room is my telescope, pointing up out of the attic skylight. Mum and Dad bought me this for my last birthday to help me keep an eye on any dangerous asteroids that might be heading toward Earth. I follow Asteroid Watch on Twitter to get any early warnings. You can't be too careful. Mum says that it was a mega-asteroid strike that wiped the dinosaurs out, and there are thousands of asteroids in space. One could be heading straight for us right now, so I've got to keep watching the skies.

That was the one good thing about moving back to Clackthorpe. The village is right in the middle of a Dark

Sky Park that covers most of the moors. This means there's no streetlamps, no light pollution—nothing to stop you from seeing thousands of stars in the sky.

You should really set your telescope up outside to get the best results, but the cold air made Mum start coughing like crazy, so instead we used to sit up in my room together to stargaze.

I close my eyes as I remember Mum sitting on the edge of my bed, snuggled up in the fluffy dressing gown I'd bought her last Christmas, then two sizes too big for her after all her treatments at the hospital. As my new telescope spun around the sky, Mum told me about the wonders we can see. Comets and meteors, the Orion Nebula and the Andromeda galaxy, the ice rings of Saturn, and Jupiter's Great Red Spot. One of my favorite sights is Omega Centauri—a cluster of ten million stars orbiting the Milky Way. When I'm staring down the eye of the telescope, this looks like a swarm of fireflies in space.

Mum told me that when you look up at the sky at night, you're actually staring into the past. Omega Centauri is over fifteen thousand light-years away. This means when I look at it through my telescope, I'm seeing the stars as they were over fifteen thousand years ago. Some of these stars might have died ages ago, but their light is still traveling toward us. Even Barnard's Star, which is one of the nearest stars to Earth, is six light-years away. That means if I want to know what this star looks like right "now," I'm going to have to wait until I finish secondary school for its light to reach me. Mum said her experiments at the Large Hadron Collider were looking billions of years into the past to take a photo of the very beginning of the universe.

If aliens in the Oort Cloud at the edge of the solar system were staring through a superpowerful telescope at Earth right now, would they be able to look through my skylight and see Mum sitting next to me on the bed?

I open my eyes and look around the empty room. Now all they'd see is the black hole she left behind, and nothing could ever fill that.

This is going to sound awful, but sometimes I wish it had been Dad who'd died instead of Mum. You see, there are tons of clips of him on YouTube, and I can even watch the box set of his TV show, but I don't have any videos of my mum. I can't just click on a video to see her face or hear her voice.

I open up my schoolbag. The only homework that matters now is finding my mum. Leaving my packed lunch on the bed, I pull out Dad's book and flip again to the page showing the zombie cat, still trapped half dead and half alive inside the box. If I want to understand how quantum physics works, then I've got to read the rest of his explanation.

But not all scientists believe that Schrödinger's cat can be dead and alive at the same time. A scientist called

Hugh Everett had a very different explanation for the strange ways that atoms behave in the quantum world. This is the many worlds interpretation. His theory said that when the box is opened, the universe splits in two. In one universe the cat is dead, and in another universe the cat is alive. Both of these parallel universes are real, and could even be in the same place in space but separated in different dimensions.

Parallel universes, different dimensions—quantum physics sounds more like science fiction than science fact.

According to the many worlds interpretation, there is an infinite number of these parallel universes, each one filled with a copy of you living an identical life, but with one tiny change where a different choice has been made. Scientists now working at the Large Hadron Collider in CERN think their experiments might even be able to detect the existence of these parallel universes by creating nano black holes.

Wait a minute! Mum never told me this. I thought her experiments at the Large Hadron Collider were all about trying to find out how the universe began, not discovering parallel ones. I look at the cardboard boxes littering my room, most of them filled with Mum's stuff from CERN.

Maybe the clue to finding a way to one of these parallel worlds is hidden in one of these boxes. . . .

Opening up the cardboard flaps, I start to unpack the nearest of the boxes. The first things I find are piles of boring-looking magazines called the *International Journal of Theoretical Physics, Nuclear Instruments and Methods in Physics Research,* and *Physics Letters.* I flip through the last of these, but it doesn't have any interesting problem pages like some of Mum's other magazines, and to be honest, I can't understand a single word.

Underneath these magazines is a pile of stuff that Mum used to keep on her desk at CERN. One by one, I pull these out of the box. There's a digital USB Geiger counter for detecting radioactivity, a Newton's cradle desk toy with its wires all tangled up, an Albert Einstein mouse pad, a laptop stand, and an old ammonite fossil.

Mum and I found this fossil when we were walking on the moors together on one of our trips back to visit Grand-dad Joe. It's about three centimeters wide, gold-colored, and shaped like a spiral. When we found it, Mum told me it was all that was left of an extinct sea creature that lived 100 million years ago. Dad said he was going to make the fossil into a necklace for Mum, but he never got around to it. I put the ammonite in my pocket.

Next in the box there are more piles of paper— computer printouts filled with endless lines of strange

messages that don't make any sense. DECAY ACTI-
VATED AT BEAMPIPE AND LEVEL 1. IONIZATION
ACTIVE IN 2 MAIN VOLUME. I don't know what any
of this means. I don't know what I'm looking for. I'm not a
quantum physicist—I'm only in Year 6.

My initial burst of hope starts to fade away. If Mum
couldn't find a parallel universe, then what chance do I
have? But as I pull out the last of the papers, I see the answer to my prayers at the bottom of the box. It's a leather
shoulder bag—the one that my mum took with her to
work every day.

I unzip it and pull out Mum's laptop. She brought this
back from CERN when she thought she could carry on
working from home—before the first blast of radiotherapy
left her too weak to eat, let alone work.

Mum told me that her laptop was a prototype quantum
computer, millions of times more powerful than any ordinary laptop you'd find in PC World. You see, Mum's laptop
is linked to the Grid—a huge network of computers dotted
around the world. The Grid analyzes the billions of tons of
data churned out by the Large Hadron Collider every time
it smashes atoms together. Most ordinary computers would
take years to analyze each collision, but Mum's quantum
supercomputer can do this in seconds. It's even got its own
mini particle accelerator on a computer chip inside—a mi-
cro Large Hadron Collider—that can virtually replay the
results of her experiments. Nanotechnology, Mum said,

and even Dad looked impressed when he saw it for the first time.

I open the laptop, the screen blinking into life almost before I press the button to turn it on. A stream of zeroes and ones pulses across the screen, flashing by so quickly that they all blur into one. This is the data streaming in from the Large Hadron Collider. If Dad's book is right, the proof that parallel universes are real is hidden somewhere inside this.

This is when I have my eureka moment.

Scientists say "Eureka!" whenever they think up amazing new theories. It was all started by this scientist called Archimedes who lived in ancient Greece over two thousand years ago. Apparently he had some brilliant idea when he was jumping into the bath, and then ran around in the nude shouting "Eureka!" I think it's an old Greek word that means "I found it," or maybe just "I'm freezing cold!"

Anyway, I don't start running around Clackthorpe in the nude, but as I look at the empty cardboard box and the flickering laptop screen, I have my own brilliant idea.

On his TV show, Dad once said that the greatest scientific discoveries are made when a scientist looks at something and thinks, "I wonder what will happen if I change this a bit."

That's what an experiment is.

So if Schrödinger's cat could be sent into a parallel universe when it was put in a box with a lump of radioactive uranium, a Geiger counter, and a bottle of poison, what would happen if I climbed into the box instead? Obviously I don't want to turn up in a parallel world as dead as a dodo, so I can ditch the bottle of poison. I've already got my mum's digital USB Geiger counter, but looking around my room, I can't see any lumps of radioactive uranium. I do, however, spot my packed lunch.

One cheese-and-pickle sandwich, a bag of potato chips, and a banana.

Do you know that bananas are radioactive? Take a look at the fruit bowl in your kitchen. If there's a banana in there, chances are it's just given you a dose of radioactivity. Don't worry, this doesn't mean you're going to turn bright green if you take a bite. You'd have to eat about five million bananas to turn into a mutant zombie. It's radioactive because in addition to all the vitamins you find in normal fruit like apples and pears, bananas have a secret ingredient called potassium-40. This means that at any moment, there's a 10 percent chance that a banana will give you a blast of gamma ray radiation when an atom inside it decays.

I grab the banana from my bed and put it next to the laptop, digital USB Geiger counter, and cardboard box on the floor. If there's a 10 percent chance of the banana going radioactive, then according to Dad's book, this should split the universe in two. In one universe the banana will sit there harmlessly, while in the other it will spit out a radioactive gamma ray. If I hook up the Geiger counter to Mum's quantum computer, then maybe it can find a shortcut to the parallel universe where this happens. I decide to call this the Quantum Banana Theory.

Pulling the box on its side to make it easier to climb inside, I plug the Geiger counter into the laptop's USB port. Then I put both of these and the banana inside the box.

Peering inside, I can see the digital readout on the Geiger counter screen showing a big fat zero CPM. CPM stands for clicks per minute—the higher the level of radiation, the more clicks you get from the Geiger counter. So there's no sign yet of the banana going into meltdown. It's time to start the experiment.

I'm just about to climb inside the box when a teeny-tiny worry stops me. I know from watching my dad's TV show that loads of scientists have experimented on themselves, and it hasn't always gone well. To test his theory that lightning and electricity were the same, a scientist called Benjamin Franklin flew his kite in the middle of a thunderstorm. He proved himself right when a huge bolt of lightning hit the kite and gave him a massive electric shock! Then there was the guy who strapped himself to a rocket-powered sled to find out what would happen when a human being traveled faster than the speed of sound, and he nearly popped his eyeballs out of his head.

Experimenting on yourself can be a risky business. How can I be sure exactly what will happen to me when I close the lid of the box? I need to find a safe way to test the Quantum Banana Theory.

This is when I have my second eureka moment. Maybe Schrödinger had the right idea after all. Before I climb into a cardboard box with a radioactive banana, I need to find a cat to try it out.

THE ONLY PET I'VE EVER HAD WAS A HAMSTER called Hawking. Mum and Dad gave him to me for my tenth birthday to try to make up for the move back to Clackthorpe. Dad suggested his name, although I sometimes called him Hawkeye because I thought that sounded cooler.

Unfortunately, next door's cat—Dylan—must have thought his name was Hamburger, because when I set up a hamster run for Hawking in the back garden, Dylan jumped over the fence and ate him. I'd only turned my back for a second, but when I turned around, Dylan was in the middle of the run munching on my hamster. When she heard me shout, Mum rushed out to try to get Dylan to drop him, but by the time he did, it was too late for Hawking.

It's funny—I think I cried more when Hawking died than I did when Mum passed away. It's not that I loved my hamster more than my mum. To be honest, he was a bit annoying sometimes when he was chugging around his squeaky wheel when I was trying to get to sleep. I think it was because when I saw him on the grass after Dylan had stalked off, I realized there wasn't anything I could do to put things right. Not like now.

Dylan belongs to Mrs. Carrington—the crazy old lady who lives next door. You never see a bird land in our back garden anymore out of fear that Dylan might be lurking somewhere in the bushes, waiting to pounce. And as for any sparrows too stupid to read the BEWARE OF THE CAT sign on Mrs. Carrington's back gate, the only sign they leave behind is a ketchup smear on the grass while Dylan prowls around picking feathers out of his teeth.

Dylan's even got a feline behavior order from the council. It says he has to be kept indoors on Tuesday mornings when the trash collectors are on their rounds. This is because Dylan scalped one of them with his claws when he disturbed him taking a nap on top of a recycling bin. Mrs. Carrington came around to our house to complain about this and tried to get Mum and Dad to sign a petition to give Dylan back his freedom, but Dad was just about to take Mum to the hospital and told Mrs. Carrington he had more important things to worry about.

When NASA decided to fly to the moon, they chose the toughest test pilots who would be able to survive the journey. If I was looking for a cat to test the Quantum Banana Theory, then Dylan was the number one candidate. The only problem: how would I get Dylan inside the box?

On top of the pile of books next to my bed is one of my favorite books ever: *Snake Mason's Guide to Wild Survival*. It's the tie-in book to my favorite TV show—*Wild Survival*. Snake Mason is an adventurer who travels the world showing celebrities how to survive in the wild. He's taught pop singers how to wrestle crocodiles, caught poisonous snakes with Premier League footballers, and rescued reality TV stars from man-eating tigers. If I want to catch Dylan and live to tell the tale, then I need to follow the advice in Snake's book.

Flipping through the pages, I find a plan to catch a Bengal tiger by digging a trapping pit. This is a deep pit in the ground covered with branches and leaves as camouflage. When the Bengal tiger takes a stroll through the jungle, it steps onto the camouflaged branches and falls right into the trap. In the book, Snake says this is one of the best ways to catch a dangerous big cat.

Now I could dig a pit in the back garden, cover it with branches and leaves, and just wait for Dylan to take his usual prowl across the lawn to pee in the flower beds and fall right into my trap. But I don't think I'm going to be able to do this without Granddad Joe spotting me, and besides, Dad would go nuts if I dug up the lawn.

So it's the second part of Snake's plan that catches my attention.

To help you capture this dangerous tiger, you need to lay a trail. Wild boar, goats, and deer can be used as bait to tempt the tiger into your trap.

I don't think they make wild boar–flavored kibble, and the only goats and deer near here are at Stormbridge Wildlife Park. But maybe I can find something in the kitchen that will help me tempt Dylan inside the box.

Heading downstairs, I hear Granddad Joe snoring. I look inside the living room and see him fast asleep in his armchair, mouth open wide, while on the TV Doc Brown shows Marty McFly his DeLorean time machine. No need now to explain to Granddad Joe why I'm looking for cat food, not popcorn.

I know from the pets project we did in school that there's a ton of food cats can't eat. Chocolate, cheese, chewing gum—they're all the ones I know, because Miss Benjamin gave me the letter C to research. I can't remember the other ones, but as I look through the kitchen cupboards in search of cat treats, I don't want to risk picking something that's going to poison Dylan. Not before he's had a chance to test out the Quantum Banana Theory.

I find what I'm looking for at the back of the cereal cupboard. A packet of LolCat Treatz with Chicken. Mum bought these when Mrs. Carrington asked us to look after Dylan while she was going to visit her sister up in Hull. But then the Hawking incident happened, and Mum told Mrs. Carrington that she didn't think we could look after Dylan after all, given the circumstances. Mrs. Carrington told Mum that I shouldn't have let my hamster run wild in the back garden and that Dylan probably thought he was a rat. They didn't talk much after that.

On the side of the packet it says *Every cat's a LolCat when it eats these tasty treats. Shake the packet and watch your cat come running!* I only hope they're tasty enough to tempt Dylan to follow my trail.

Back up in my bedroom, I check that everything is in the right place. I move the cardboard box so it's facing the door—still on its side so that Dylan can easily climb in. At the back of the box, my mum's laptop is still hooked up to the Geiger counter, the banana propped in front of it. Everything is ready—except me.

Now, obviously I'm not going to try to catch Dylan the psycho cat without some kind of protection. When Snake Mason captured the man-eating tigers of the Sundarbans, he wore a camouflage Kevlar bodysuit and a helmet with a face painted on the back because tigers usually attack you from behind. I have to make do with a pair of gardening gloves, my old BMX body armor that is now two sizes too small, and a scary clown Halloween mask worn back to front. I look ridiculous, but if it keeps me safe from Dylan's claws, I don't care.

With the packet of LolCat Treatz in my gloved hand, I step out into the back garden. I'm ready to start laying my trail.

Little bubbles of excitement are fizzing inside my stomach, and I can't stop a tiny burp from slipping out. If this works, then I'm one step closer to finding my mum.

I decide to put the first treat at the bottom of the garden path. This is right next to the shed, or what my dad likes to call his workshop, although he never goes in there now, as he spends all his time working down in the Deep Mine Lab. This is one of the places where Dylan likes to hide in the flower beds—jumping out to ambush any birds that make the mistake of landing in our garden.

This time, though, there's no sign of Dylan lurking in the undergrowth and the only sound I can hear is a bee buzzing over the rosebushes. Now, Snake Mason says that the most dangerous sound you'll ever hear in the jungle is silence. This is a sign that a big predator is on the prowl and all the other animals have fled real quick. So when even the bee stops buzzing, some sixth sense for danger makes me turn around to see Dylan crouching in front of the shed, ready to pounce.

As I slowly back away, Dylan eyes the first of the Lol-

Cat Treatz that I've dropped on the path. To me these look more like something a cat leaves behind than something it'd want to eat, but Dylan must think differently, as he arches his back and pounces on the treat. One second it's there, and the next it's gone.

Licking his lips, Dylan turns his attention back to me. He seems to have a fresh swagger in his prowl as he steps toward me. Beneath my BMX body armor, I can feel my heart thudding in my chest.

"Nice kitty," I say, slowly backing away. I shake another treat into the palm of my gardening glove. A single one weighs three grams, and this packet of LolCat Treatz says it contains sixty grams of treats. This means I've got nineteen left. I've measured the distance from the cardboard box in my bedroom to Dad's shed, and it's thirty meters. This means I can give Dylan one LolCat treat every one and a half meters.

Down the garden path, through the kitchen, and up the stairs past the sound of Granddad Joe's snores, I carefully shake out the tasty chicken treats, Dylan gobbling up each one with a snap of his jaws. The packet in my hand is getting lighter with every step I take, and as Dylan slinks up the final step to my bedroom, I only hope I've got enough left to get him into the box.

Inside the cardboard box I can see the glow of the laptop screen and the blur of flashing zeroes and ones lighting up the Geiger counter. No sound of any clicking yet to tell me the banana is going radioactive. I tip the last of the LolCat Treatz into my hand. There are only two left.

Dylan stops dead in his tracks, his hackles rising as the door swings shut behind his tail.

I'm now trapped in my bedroom with a psychopathic cat.

Opening my trembling hand, I show Dylan the last of the LolCat Treatz, then throw them into the open cardboard box with a flick of my wrist.

Dylan doesn't need to be asked twice. With a flash of fur he springs forward into the box. Quickly I push the cardboard flaps shut behind him, pressing my weight against the lid as I prepare myself for the inevitable feline explosion when Dylan discovers he's trapped.

From inside the box I hear the faint clicking of the Geiger counter, followed by a puzzled meow. Then this meow is suddenly cut off into silence like a cat being pushed out of a spaceship airlock.

I wait for a moment, trying to work out if Dylan has just got a frog (or a hamster) in his throat. Maybe he's playing dead to try to fool me into opening the box. But as the seconds tick on, I can't hear a single sound from inside. Not even the faint click of the Geiger counter.

Tensing myself, I slowly open the cardboard flaps, ready for Dylan to spring out, claws first. But when I look inside the box, all I can see is the laptop, the banana, and the Geiger counter. There is no cat. Dylan has disappeared.

My brain tries to work out exactly what this means. When Schrödinger put his cat in a box with a lump of radioactive uranium and a bottle of poison, he knew that it was going to end up either dead or alive—or maybe even both at the same time. But unless Dylan's been vaporized by a radioactive banana, there's only one explanation for what's happened here. The Quantum Banana Theory works, and Dylan is now in a parallel universe.

I stare into the box, the zeroes and ones still scrolling across the laptop screen. My head's buzzing with excitement. This isn't a box anymore—this is a door to another dimension. And on the other side of that door, my mum could be waiting for me.

There's no time to waste. It's time to try the experiment again—this time with me as the subject. Climbing into the box, I pull my knees up to my chest to fit inside. It's a tight squeeze, but I just about manage it. I reach forward and pull the flaps of the box closed behind me. All I've got to do now is wait for the banana to spit out a radioactive gamma ray, and then the universe will split into two.

My stomach makes a groaning noise like the TARDIS taking off. It must be nerves, or maybe I shouldn't have skipped lunch. In the light from the laptop screen, I can see the banana resting against the Geiger counter, and although my stomach's still rumbling, I don't think it would be a good idea to eat part of the experiment.

I feel like an astronaut sitting in a rocket as the countdown reaches zero. Adrenaline is racing around inside me, and it's all I can do to keep myself sitting still.

Downstairs, Granddad Joe is probably still asleep in front of *Back to the Future*, while Dad is in his underground lab pretending that everything's OK by trying to solve the mysteries of the universe. Me? I'm actually doing it. I'm going to find Mum again.

That's when I hear the clicking noise—the telltale sound of the Geiger counter that means a radioactive particle in the banana has just decayed. I tense up waiting for the universe to split into two. I've watched loads of science fiction films, so I'm expecting the box to start shaking itself to bits with flashing lights and some seriously impressive special effects, but all I get is a beep from my mum's laptop and then the clicking stops.

Is that it?

Nervously I push open the lid of the box and peer outside. I can see my telescope still pointing up out the skylight, and piles of books, comics, and cardboard boxes cluttering up the floor. With a sinking feeling, I climb out of the box.

Nothing has changed. There's my desk and swivel chair, the map of the solar system still stuck up above my bed. It hasn't worked.

I can feel my eyes starting to leak. Dad was wrong. Quantum physics is a load of rubbish. Parallel universes don't exist. You only get one world. You only get one mum. And I'm never going to get to see mine again.

I rub my eyes angrily, and that's when I notice something's not quite right.

On the poster of the solar system above my bed, there should be eight planets lined up from left to right: Mercury, Venus, Earth, Mars, Jupiter, Saturn, Uranus, and Neptune. But this poster seems to show nine instead.

I shake my head, thinking I must have rubbed my eyes too hard, but when I look again, there's still a brand-new planet between Mars and Jupiter.

I stare at the poster in disbelief, trying to make sense of it. Instead of the asteroid belt, there's a bright-purple planet hanging in space where no planet should be. The caption on the poster gives me its name. Ceres.

When I realize what this means, I can't stop myself from smiling. Dad's book said that in a parallel universe there might just be one tiny change. Well, I reckon a brand-new planet in the solar system must count as a pretty big one. The Quantum Banana Theory really works. I must be in a parallel universe.

"What the—"

The sound of my own voice makes me spin around. Standing in front of me I see—well, me. The same face, the same hair, the same school uniform. It's like looking into a mirror, except this Albie isn't wearing BMX body armor, gardening gloves, and a scary clown Halloween mask worn back to front.

I open my mouth to start to explain exactly who I am, how I've traveled from a parallel universe, and how everything's going to be OK now.

And that's when this other Albie punches me in the face.

SIR ISAAC NEWTON INVENTED GRAVITY. WELL, he didn't invent it, but he definitely discovered it. One minute he was sitting under a tree minding his own business, and the next minute an apple fell down out of the tree and conked him on the head. Most normal people would just think "Ouch!" or "Why did I decide to sit under this flipping tree?" But Sir Isaac Newton was a scientist, and instead he wondered why apples always fall down and not up.

Newton worked out that gravity was the reason why, and he came up with his three laws of motion to describe how things move scientifically. Newton's third law of motion says that for every action there is an equal and opposite reaction. So when this parallel-universe Albie hits me in the face, I end up hitting the floor.

Now, it's not like he knocks me out with a single punch, but when I step back in surprise at being hit in the face, I trip over a pile of comics, bang my head on the edge of the desk, and knock myself right out.

When I open my eyes again, I discover I've been duct-taped to a swivel chair by my evil twin from a parallel universe who's now leaning over me holding a compass set. And from the expression on his face, it doesn't look as though he's planning to use it in a very mathematical way.

"What are you doing in my bedroom?" he says, menacingly jabbing the compass in my direction.

I try to explain how I've used a quantum computer, a Geiger counter, and a banana to travel from another universe inside a cardboard box. How I'm searching for my mum and to make everything right again. I even want to ask if he's seen my next-door neighbor's cat, but with the duct tape over my mouth, this all comes out more like "mff-SMURGLE-FLURGLE-GURGLE-mff!"

My arms and legs are wrapped in duct tape too, pinning me to the chair. I try to pull myself free, but this just spins the chair and I end up tipping myself sideways.

This other Albie leans forward, the point of his compass now dangerously close to several of my vital organs, as well as a few others that probably aren't so vital but that I'm still kind of attached to. In my chest my heart is beating faster than an atom whizzing around the Large Hadron

Collider. OK, maybe not quite that fast, as that would re-sult in a serious heart attack, but fast enough to show that I'm pretty freaked out by the whole situation.

It's not because I'm scared, although the compass is definitely keeping me on my toes. It's the total weirdness of seeing my own face staring back at me. You might think that you see your own face in the mirror every day, but you never see your face in the same way as everybody else does. The face you see in the mirror is reversed. If you've got a spot on your right cheek, in the mirror it looks like it's on the left. Try it yourself—hold this book up to a mirror and you'll see the words on the page are the wrong way around. So this was the first time I'd ever had the chance to see what I *really* look like. And to tell you the truth, it's kind of creepy.

This parallel-universe Albie—I'll just call him Bad Albie for short—has the same green eyes, the same dark-brown hair, the same mouth and nose, and even the same mole on his cheek as me. I can even see parts of my face that you can never see properly in a mirror—like inside my ear and that bit under my chin. All these features are put together in exactly the same way, but this Albie looks dif-ferent to me. He looks mean.

"I know what you are," Bad Albie hisses, reaching up to pull the tape from my mouth. "You're a clone."

"Ow!"

Now, I should put him right straightaway, but I'm too busy checking that he hasn't ripped off half my face along with the tape.

"So this is the secret science project that my dad's been working on for the past year?" he says. "All the time he said he was working on perfecting cold fusion when really he was creating a clone of me."

As Bad Albie babbles in my ear, my stomach takes a nosedive—a delayed reaction to traveling to a parallel universe, I suppose—and I throw up all over the floor.

"Aw, no! Not on my X-Men comics."

Luckily, spewing my guts up over his comics collection convinces Bad Albie to take off the rest of the duct tape that's keeping me prisoner. After using a towel to cover up the sick, he sits on the edge of my bed—I mean, his bed—staring at me.

"You're not going to puke again, are you?" he asks. "That must be the side effect of all the cloning drugs my dad's given you."

I'm still feeling pretty sick, but I manage to shake my head in reply.

"I'm not a clone," I tell him.

Bad Albie laughs sourly.

"Of course you're a clone. Just look at you."

In my bedroom there's a mirror on the wall facing me, and as I glance up I see that this universe has got the same.

My reflection stares back with this alternate Albie sitting next to me—the two of us creating our own mirror image.

"So what was my dad's plan?" Bad Albie asks. "Create a new happy family with the real me out of the picture? Get you to kidnap me and take my place so you can play the part of the perfect son? Am I too much trouble for him now that he's the superstar scientist on every TV screen? Isn't it enough that he leaves me stuck here in this stupid village while he jets off to the White House? I know Dad said I was on my final warning after that last detention at school, but I didn't think that meant he'd replace me with a programmed clone."

My head spins as Bad Albie spits out his crazy theory. I might be in a parallel universe, but it doesn't sound like much has changed for my superstar scientist dad. But what's all this nonsense about kidnapping and clones . . .

Wait a minute. "What do you mean, '*the White House*'?"

"Durr!" Bad Albie pulls a face like he's talking to the most stupid person in the universe. "Have the cloning drugs fried your brain too? It's where the president of the United States lives." He pulls out his mobile and swipes the screen.

"Take a look. My dad tweeted this a couple of hours ago."

I look down to see a picture of Dad's face staring out from his Twitter profile.

@DrBenBright
Physicist. Philanthropist. Father.
Inventor of cold fusion. Drinker of hot coffee.

TWEETS	FOLLOWING	FOLLOWERS	LIKES
4,572	314	61.3M	37

My evil twin taps on Dad's latest tweet, which zooms out to fill the screen of his smartphone.

Ben Bright @DrBenBright • 5h
Great to have met President Cruise and announced the building of the next wave of cold fusion reactors across the USA! #CEBFoundation

Beneath this tweet is a photo of my dad in the Oval Office of the White House. He's shaking hands with someone who looks like a Hollywood film star, his broad smile dazzling the camera while my dad just pulls a geeky grin like he can't quite believe who he's shaking hands with. Neither can I.

On his TV show, Dad usually rubs shoulders with pop stars and celebrities—you know, pushing stand-up comedians wearing suits made out of Mentos into dunk tanks filled with Diet Coke. But this picture shows him shaking hands with the president of the United States in this parallel world.

I look up at Bad Albie as he swipes the photo away. I'm

beginning to realize that a brand-new planet between Mars and Jupiter isn't the only difference between his universe and mine. In this universe, Dad's Twitter profile says he's the inventor of cold fusion, but I don't have a clue what this means.

"What *is* cold fusion?"

The expression on Bad Albie's face hardens into a frown.

"Don't you know anything, Clone Boy?" he sneers. "You're not going to be able to fool anyone that you're me if you don't even know a simple fact like that. Cold fusion is my dad's brilliant invention, which should have made him a billionaire. Nuclear energy from a fusion generator the size of a microwave. The power of the stars in every home and business across the world—safe, cold, and clean. No more global warming, no more food shortages, no more poverty. Unlimited energy helping solve every problem the world has ever known. All given away for free by my dad's stupid charity—the C.E.B. Foundation."

This parallel-universe Albie is really starting to annoy me. My dad might be a scientific genius in this parallel world, but why am I such an idiot? I try to stay calm. I didn't come here to get into an argument with myself. I came here to find my mum.

"So what does Mum think about all this?" I ask him, trying to keep the sarcasm out of my voice. "Surely she's going to have something to say if she finds out Dad's planning to swap you for a clone?"

Bad Albie stares at me like I've just asked him to jump into a black hole.

"My mum's dead." He spits out the words one by one, his face flushed with anger. "She died of cancer when I was just a baby."

My heart seems to freeze in my chest. No. She can't be dead. Not here. Dad said that quantum physics proved that Mum was still alive in a parallel universe. But according to Bad Albie, this just isn't true.

"You've probably got her name stamped on the sole of your foot," he says, still staring at me with hate in his eyes. "The Charlotte Elizabeth Bright Foundation makes all my dad's inventions now—from cold fusion to clones. He said he named the charity after my mum to keep her memory alive, but he can't wait to forget about me. You're the proof of that."

I glance up at the poster of the solar system above Bad Albie's head, staring blankly into space. The bright-purple planet between Mars and Jupiter starts to blur as the tears leak from my eyes. A parallel universe might have one tiny change, Dad said, and in this universe I've got the wrong one.

The black hole in my heart aches even harder. If I had the Death Star, I'd blow this brand-new planet to smithereens. But deep down I know this wouldn't bring Mum back.

I wipe my eyes angrily. I feel like I'm losing her all over again, but this other Albie doesn't even seem to care.

Behind him I can see the cardboard box, still on its side. In the shadows at the back, endless lines of zeroes and ones scroll across the screen of Mum's laptop. It's still hooked up to the Geiger counter with the banana resting alongside it, all ready to go radioactive again. All I need to do is wait for Bad Albie to turn his back, and then I can crawl inside that box and escape from this stupid parallel universe.

But he's still staring at me, an evil grin slowly spreading across his face.

Suddenly I feel like I'm in one of those cartoons where two castaways are both starving, and one starts to imagine that the other has turned into a giant hot dog. At least, that's the way Bad Albie seems to be looking at me now.

"What?" I ask him, still trying to work out how quickly I can get inside the box.

"If my dad's made a clone to keep me in line, then you better start earning your keep," he says. "If he wants me to behave myself at school, then *you* can go to school for me instead."

I stare back at him in disbelief. No way. I haven't traveled to a parallel universe just to go back to school. I glance back at the cardboard box, trying to work out if I can dive past my evil twin to make my escape. There's no way I'd even have time to get the lid shut.

"I can't," I tell him. "I can't go to school for you." I babble out the words as my brain whirrs, trying to think up excuses. "It's like you said—I don't know anything. How am I supposed to convince everyone that I'm you?"

"You're a *clone*," Bad Albie tells me with a hint of menace in his voice. "That's what clones do—pretend to be something they're not. If my dad wants a perfect son, then you can be the one who's top of the class. Meanwhile, I get to stay here and take it easy."

He picks the compass up off the desk and waggles it in my direction.

"Anyway, you're already dressed the part—once you take that stupid back-to-front mask and body armor off. I thought Dad had thrown that away last year when he swapped my BMX bike for a hover scooter."

I open my mouth to protest but then quickly close it again as Bad Albie prods the point of the compass against the front of my BMX vest.

"Let's see how you like being me, Clone Boy."

I STOMP TOWARD CLACKTHORPE PRIMARY, making sure to step on every crack in the pavement. On my back is Bad Albie's rucksack, which he'd shoved in my hands as he forced me out of the house at compass point. In my mind there's a whirl of bad words, all of which would get me suspended from school if they bubbled out of my mouth.

As I look around, I try to work out how I've ended up trapped in this nightmare. The streets all look the same. The houses all look the same. Every car is parked in exactly the same place as I see them every day on the short walk to school. I turn left at the end of Sharman Street and carry on down Appleton Drive before turning right on Priestley Avenue, where the gates of Clackthorpe Primary are waiting for me on the other side of the road.

Everything is the same. Every single thing. And in this stupid universe my mum is still dead.

It's only when I start to cross the road that I notice the first big difference. A screech of brakes and the sudden blare of a car horn make me nearly jump out of my skin.

"Stupid kid! What do you think you're doing?"

As my heart hammers in my mouth, I look to my left to see an angry-looking man leaning out the window of his white van.

"Don't they teach how to cross the road in that school of yours? I could've run right over you."

I'm totally confused. I'd looked right, then left, then right again, but this van had come out of nowhere and was driving completely on the wrong side of the road.

"But—but—"

But before I can even start to protest, I see another car pull up behind the man in the van, and then a scooter whizzes past on the other side of the street. Left to right, right to left—they're all driving on the wrong side of the road.

I shake my head in confusion, trying to work out why everyone in Clackthorpe has suddenly forgotten how to drive. Then I remember what my dad's book said. *One tiny change . . .*

Of course! In this parallel universe, people must drive on the opposite side. That's why I never saw the van until it nearly knocked me down.

As the car behind beeps its horn, I lift my hand in apology, then make sure I look both ways before I cross to the safety of the school gates.

"Keep your head out of the clouds next time you're crossing the road," White Van Man shouts after me as he steps on the accelerator. "Remember you're on planet Earth with the rest of us."

As I race across the empty playground, I only wish I knew which one.

When I open the door to Class 6, I can see that I'm late—again. The rest of the class is already sitting at their desks as Miss Benjamin takes attendance.

"Kiran?"

"Yes, miss."

"Olivia?"

"Here, miss."

I nervously scan the classroom, searching for any tiny changes in the faces of Class 6. Everybody looks exactly the same. I try to catch Kiran's eye as he sits in our usual place near the front of the class, but he just stares right through me.

"Albie?" Miss Benjamin calls out.

"Here, miss," I reply automatically, and it's when she turns in her chair to face me that I get my next surprise.

She's old. I mean, seriously ancient. In my universe Miss Benjamin is already getting on a bit—I think she must be at least twenty-five or twenty-six. But in this parallel universe, she's got wrinkles all around her eyes, and I can see a nest of gray hairs poking out beneath her dyed blond hair.

"You're late, Albie," she says, tapping her watch impatiently. "Again."

I stare back at Miss Benjamin in disbelief. How come the rest of my class looks exactly the same, but my teacher looks like she's been run over by a time machine?

"Don't just stand there, Albie," she sighs. "What on earth is the matter with you?"

The words jump out of my mouth before my brain has a chance to call them back.

"Miss, you're so old."

This is so not the right thing to say. As a wave of laughter runs around the classroom, Miss Benjamin's left eye begins to twitch beneath her crow's feet.

"Sit down, Albie," she snaps. "Or else you'll find yourself working in the head teacher's office while the rest of Class Six comes with me on our trip to the museum."

My heart sinks even as my face turns red. My teacher might have become geriatric, and there might be a brand-new planet between Mars and Jupiter, but somehow it still seems like the only school trip that Class 6 ever takes is to the Clackthorpe Museum of Natural History and Mechanical Wonders.

Keeping my head down as Miss Benjamin calls out the

next name, I make a beeline for my usual place: sitting right next to Kiran. But when I sit down, Kiran stares at me like I've got two heads or something.

"What are you doing?" he hisses.

"What do you mean?" I whisper back, keeping my voice low to avoid another rocket from Miss Benjamin. "It's me—Albie."

"You know you're not allowed to sit next to me," Kiran replies, frowning so hard it looks like his forehead could give Miss Benjamin's wrinkles a run for their money. "It's in your behavior contract."

At the start of each term, Miss Benjamin gives everyone in Class 6 a behavior contract. This tells you the rules she wants you to follow in school—things like no calling out, no chatting when the teacher is talking, and no making sudden loud noises in the classroom. Most people just get two or three rules to follow, although Wesley MacNamara's behavior contract covers four sides of A4 paper. But I don't know why Bad Albie's says I'm not allowed to sit next to my best friend in school.

All my frustration at everything that's gone wrong since I climbed out of the cardboard box in this stupid universe suddenly rises to the surface.

"That's ridiculous," I tell Kiran while Miss Benjamin continues to take attendance. "Why does she want to stop us from sitting next to each other?"

"Because I asked her to," my best friend snaps in reply.

"It's your fault I got the blame when you let Mr. Sniffles out of his cage. When he jumped out of the classroom window and got eaten by that mad cat that just appeared out of nowhere, I was the one who got put in detention."

Wait a minute! This isn't right. It was Wesley MacNamara who let Mr. Sniffles out of his cage—not me—and Miss Benjamin stopped him before he escaped out the window. Except in this parallel universe it must have been Bad Albie . . .

"And if it wasn't for you I'd have won first prize at the science fair," Kiran says with a scowl, "but you thought it'd be a laugh to pop my balloons before I even had the chance to launch my mission into space."

I shake my head. I wouldn't do that—not to my best friend.

"And now you want to get me involved in this crazy scheme, just so you've got someone to pin the blame on when it all goes wrong."

"I don't know what you mean." I'm getting more confused with every new thing Kiran says. "What crazy scheme?"

Kiran gives me a look like I've just farted in the airlock of the International Space Station.

"Just leave me alone, Albie," he hisses. "I don't want to be your friend anymore."

Kiran is my best friend in Class 6. He's my only friend

in Class 6. Or at least, he used to be, in another universe. Just when I think things can't get any worse, this parallel world proves me wrong again.

When I was little, Mum and Dad took me to the funfair in Geneva. We had a great time going on the bumper cars, the pirate ships, and even the ghost train, but everything went wrong when I got lost in the hall of mirrors. One minute Mum and I were together, laughing at our funny reflections, and then I raced ahead to see what was around the corner and when I looked back she was gone. All I could see were endless copies of myself.

Everything was twisted. Nothing looked right. My own face distorted into something terrifying that I couldn't even recognize. It must've been less than a minute until Mum found me again, but I'll never forget how scared I was.

That's how I feel now. Everything is twisted and wrong. I don't recognize the Albie Bright in this universe. What's happened to turn him into such an idiot?

Then I remember he's lost his mum. Just like me, but for Bad Albie it happened when he was just a baby. Is this what's made him twisted inside? And if it is, does that mean I'm going to turn into an idiot too?

All I want to do is crawl back inside the cardboard box in my bedroom and hope that the Quantum Banana Theory can get me out of this place. But there's no chance of that now, as Miss Benjamin snaps the attendance book shut, pulling my attention back to a more immediate problem.

"Right, Class Six, we're heading off to the museum, and I want you all to be on your very best behavior." Her left eye twitches as she scans the class, her surprising wrinkles creasing into a frown as her gaze settles on me. "And that includes you, Albie Bright. Now, line up outside sensibly and then we'll be on our way."

Whenever Miss Benjamin takes us on a class trip, she always makes us walk in a crocodile. This doesn't mean she uses her shape-shifting extraterrestrial powers to turn us all into green, scaly amphibious reptiles with extra-large teeth—although Wesley MacNamara would probably be pretty impressed if she did. When we walk in a crocodile, Miss Benjamin leads the way and we all have to follow behind in a line, walking in pairs with our crocodile buddy.

Kiran is usually my crocodile buddy, so I'm feeling more than a little bit lost as I watch him line up in the playground with Timothy Chase. As Miss Benjamin goes down the line checking the crocodile, it seems like everyone in Class 6 is already paired up. I'm starting to panic that I'm going to end up holding hands with my antique teacher when, from out of nowhere, Victoria Barnes slips her arm through mine.

"Looking for a new crocodile buddy?" she asks, tossing her long blond hair back over her shoulder like an apprentice supermodel. "Or is my boyfriend too cool to walk me to his dad's museum?"

My jaw drops to the ground, but no words come out. This is because my brain has just been put on a spin cycle, and all my thoughts are sloshing about inside my head at triple speed. Victoria Barnes is holding my hand. The most popular girl in school has just told me that I'm her boyfriend. What fresh weirdness is this?

My malfunctioning brain sends a message to my mouth, and I find myself repeating Victoria's words at random like a printer with a system error.

"Boyfriend—walk—museum."

My face quickly turns red as I realize how stupid this sounds, but Victoria just laughs as though she's in on the joke.

"Me boyfriend. Me walk," she says, putting on a cartoon caveman voice. "You're so funny, Albie." Then she gives my hand a little squeeze.

This just makes my face turn even redder. I think I preferred it when she was calling me lamebrain.

At the front of the line, Miss Benjamin signals the crocodile into motion.

"Right, Class Six—follow me, and don't forget your Green Cross Code."

Miss Benjamin turns right as she leads us out of the playground, the crocodile following in line behind. Other schools get to go to London to visit the Natural History Museum or take a trip to Manchester to explore the Museum of Science and Industry, but Class 6 just gets to walk halfway down the street to see the Clackthorpe Museum of Natural History and Mechanical Wonders.

But I don't have any time now to grumble about the quality of our extracurricular activities, because Victoria hits me with another question.

"So, are you ready for my birthday party tomorrow?" she says, her blue eyes glittering with excitement. "It's going to be *so* amazing. Don't forget—it starts at seven in the village hall. There's going to be a DJ, a photo booth, and you won't guess what else."

This is all sounding strangely familiar to me.

"A dance competition?"

"Yes!" Victoria replies, a look of triumph on her face. "We're *so* going to win that!"

"But I can't dance," I protest, forgetting in my panic that there's no chance of me hanging around for Victoria's party.

"Don't worry, I came in third in the regional heats of the Search for a Junior Dance Star competition," she tells me, fluttering her eyelids in false modesty. "My tango got top marks. And wait until you see the gorgeous new dress Mum has bought me—that old red thing with sequins just made me look like a tomato."

The only time I've ever danced is around the kitchen

with my mum. When Dad was away, Mum would play her favorite tunes from when they first met, and together we'd work out crazy dance steps while we were eating our pizzas. There was one song I remember where Mum busted out what she called her "old-school hip-hop moves," putting her Higgs boson baseball cap on backward as she rapped along with the intergalactic tune. I ended up laughing so hard that pizza came out of my nose.

"What's the matter?" Victoria asks, noticing before me that my eyes have started to leak.

"It's just hay fever," I tell her quickly, reaching into my pocket for a tissue to wipe the memories away.

The crocodile comes to a halt at the front of the museum, and it's when I finish wiping my eyes that I get my next big surprise.

In my universe, the Clackthorpe Museum of Natural History and Mechanical Wonders is in an old detached house that looks more like a dusty antique shop or the kind of run-down hotel you usually see in a horror film.

But the huge building in front of me is made of glass and steel, all sharp angles and straight lines rising up into the sky like an alien spaceship that's taken a wrong turn at Mars and landed in Clackthorpe by mistake. I rub my eyes, certain that this time I must be dreaming. But the spaceship doesn't take off, and instead I see the sign above the entrance as Miss Benjamin begins to lead Class 6 inside.

FUSION
SPONSORED BY THE C.E.B. FOUNDATION
Formerly the Clackthorpe Museum of Natural History
and Mechanical Wonders

As Victoria rushes to follow the others with a squeal of
excitement, I suddenly feel a long way from home.

"WELCOME TO FUSION."

My jaw drops in surprise as Dad greets me and the rest of Class 6 as we wait in the huge entrance hall.

"In this immersive museum, you'll discover the secrets of the universe. Do you dare to stare into the mirror of infinity? Or take a spin at nearly the speed of light around the Large Hadron Collider? From the Chillerator, where you'll learn how cold fusion uses the power of the stars, to the Dark Matter Detector, where you'll search for the secret ingredient of space itself, every interactive exhibit will help you learn how science can explain the wonders of the universe."

Of course it's only a hologram. A life-size 3-D image of my dad beamed onto a raised platform at the entrance to the museum. The real thing is on the other side of the Atlantic Ocean, probably thinking about eating breakfast at the White House, but the hologram looks so realistic that I can't stop myself from reaching out to touch it.

"Albie!" Miss Benjamin's voice rings out with a warning note.

A pattern of colored dots crawls over my skin as the image of Dad's hand passes through my own, the beams of light coming together to create the hologram. It's just a cheap trick to make you think that Professor Ben Bright is really here. Even in this parallel universe, the only way I get to see my dad is virtually.

"Before you leave, you'll even have the chance to invent your own experiment in the Eureka Zone." The hologram of my dad looks straight at me now, his face suddenly serious. "Who knows? You might even make a discovery that could change the universe."

I think about the Quantum Banana Theory—my mum's laptop hooked up to the Geiger counter as the banana inside the cardboard box slowly turns brown. *I already have, Dad. I just can't tell you about it because you're not here.*

As my dad's hologram fades away, Miss Benjamin claps her hands to keep our attention.

"Right, Class Six. I want you to think about the questions we've been exploring in class. Where does energy come from? What is matter made of? How fast is light? This morning you're going to get active to discover the answers to all these questions and more. Work in your color-coded groups to explore the exhibits, and then we'll all meet back together at twelve in the Collider Cafe to share what we've found out."

This is the signal that Class 6 has been waiting for. With a buzz of excitement, everyone swarms off to try to find the most thrilling and potentially dangerous exhibits. Beneath the spectacular glass roof, the museum's huge hall looks like a gigantic science theme park. Atom-shaped pods zoom in opposite directions around an elevated race-track that loops around the museum, zipping past each other at high speed. Fluorescent rainbow-colored columns gurgle multicolored bubbles into the air, each one popped by a giant pin that swings back and forth. I can see robot exoskeletons and dinosaurs, space probes and steam engines, an imitation volcano, and something called the Big Bang Simulator. Glass bridges and galleries lead from one zone to the next, neon signposts directing you to the Clone Zone, the Cosmic Space, the Invention Station, and loads more amazing-sounding places.

This must be the best museum in the world. And it's in Clackthorpe.

"Catch you later," Victoria says, giving me a peck on the cheek. "I'm going for a ride on the Large Hadron Collider with Olivia and Kim."

Somewhere inside my brain, my blush switch is suddenly flicked to maximum beet. Grabbing hold of her friends' hands, Victoria disappears in the direction of the atomic racetrack, leaving me looking like I've just landed from Mars.

I don't know which color-coded group I belong to. I don't know why Victoria Barnes thinks I'm her boyfriend. And as I look around the museum, I don't really know what I'm doing here.

"Come along, Albie," Miss Benjamin snaps, clicking her fingers together. "Your partner in the Gray group is waiting to get started."

There's only one other person in Class 6 who hasn't rushed off already to explore the museum.

Standing next to Miss Benjamin, Wesley MacNamara is wearing a sly smile on his face. That's when I realize I really hate this stupid universe.

"Where are we going?" I ask nervously as I follow Wesley along the empty gallery that skirts the edge of the entrance hall. "All the cool stuff is back that way."

"I've found it," he replies, tapping the side of his nose as if keeping a big secret. "We can put the plan into action."

"What plan?" I ask, feeling even more confused as I look around the deserted space. There are no dynamic demonstrations, electrifying experiments, or interactive exhibits anywhere to be seen in this corner of the museum. I don't know how we're going to find out the answers to any of Miss Benjamin's questions here. I glance back over my shoulder to see my antique teacher deep in conversation with one of the museum staff, his bright-red jacket emblazoned with the logo of the C.E.B. Foundation.

At the back of my mind I can't help worrying that Wesley is trying to lure me to a lonely part of the museum so that he can subject me to a grisly science experiment. But at least he hasn't given me a dead arm—yet.

"Operation Platypus," Wesley replies with an evil grin. "Don't try to pretend you've forgotten our brilliant plan."

Oh no, don't tell me that the Wesley MacNamara in this parallel universe is as crazy as the one I've left behind. I'd forgotten all about his failed science project to dissect a duck-billed platypus. I remember the pictures of the stuffed animals I'd seen on the website of the Clackthorpe Museum of Natural History and Mechanical Wonders. Surely there's no space for a pickled platypus in this high-tech theme park?

The sign above the frosted glass doors at the end of the gallery gives me the answer to this question.

THE MONTAGUE WILKES WING
HOME OF THE WORLD'S FINEST COLLECTION
OF ANTIQUARIAN ANIMALS
CLOSED FOR REFURBISHMENT

"Come on." Wesley grins, pushing the door open. "Let's go catch a platypus."

I freeze, trying to think of a way to get out of Wesley's crazy scheme as he slips inside the Montague Wilkes Wing. Looking back along the gallery, I can see the rest of Class 6 having fun inside the museum. I spot Kiran bouncing inside what looks like a giant hamster ball in the Atomic Zorb Zone, while Victoria Barnes is taking a selfie with her friends in front of an erupting volcano. Even Miss Benjamin is getting in on the action as she stands inside a Clone Zone pod as the curator presses a button to print an instant 3-D copy. How have I got caught up in a platypus kidnap? If Miss Benjamin finds out . . .

This is the moment when something clicks inside my brain. Since I arrived in this parallel universe, I've been duct-taped to a chair, rejected by my best friend, and even forced to hold hands with Victoria Barnes. I don't belong here, and the first chance I get I'm climbing back inside that cardboard box to escape from this crazy place.

So what does it matter if I help Wesley MacNamara steal a stupid stuffed platypus? If I get caught, the only person who's going to get the blame is the Albie Bright in this universe. Suddenly I don't feel scared anymore. I can do what I like here and get away with it scot-free.

"Albie?" Wesley's voice floats out into the gallery. "Come and look what I've found."

With a last glance over my shoulder to make sure nobody is watching, I quickly slip through the door.

Wow.

That's the only word I can use to describe what's inside.

The large room is lit by bright fluorescent lights and filled with stuffed animals of every kind. There are lions and tigers, leopards and bears, monkeys, zebras, and crocodiles. And those are just the ones I can see straightaway. But what's really creepy is that every one of these animals is dressed in clothes like it's a real person.

There's a walrus wearing a wedding dress, and it looks like it's getting married to a polar bear in a three-piece suit. A monkey in a waistcoat is riding on the back of a mountain goat, and they're both being chased by a koala in an old-fashioned car. I can see a model school filled with skunks, sitting in rows behind desks in their black-and-white uniforms. There's even a team of kangaroos playing cricket against a couple of crocodiles, all of them dressed in white sweaters. These weird scenes are displayed on platforms all around the room, each one a bit higher as the walkway curves around the exhibition.

"Pretty freaky, eh?" Wesley says, inspecting the display at the front of the room. "It says here that this Montague Wilkes guy stuffed all these animals himself to remind him of home when he was traveling around the world back in the olden days."

I'm feeling a bit homesick myself, but this spooky exhibition isn't making me feel any better. It's like a zoo where the animals have eaten all the visitors and then dressed up in their clothes.

"And there's the furry freak we're looking for," Wesley says, pointing toward the platform in the center of the room.

I look up to see an animal orchestra arranged around a stage. There are penguins playing violins, a raccoon with a bassoon, ferrets with trumpets, and an animal that looks like a civet—a small jungle cat I'd seen Snake Mason catch on *Wild Survival*—playing the clarinet. Whoever put this orchestra together really liked to give the animals an instrument that rhymes with their name.

And standing on a high podium in the center of the platform, surrounded by the stuffed musicians, is a duck-billed platypus dressed in a white tuxedo. Its flippers are spread wide and it appears to be holding a long wooden stick.

I feel a rush of adrenaline as I eye the goal of our mission. It's time to steal a platypus.

At first I don't know how we're going to get up onto the orchestra platform. The museum has put up a see-through guardrail to protect the stuffed animals from any nosy visitors—or maybe the other way around—and it's way too high to climb over. But then Wesley wheels a ladder up the walkway.

"Here we go," he says with an excited grin, pushing the ladder into position. "They must have left this out from when they were putting up the exhibits."

"Leave it to me," I tell him, putting my foot on the first

rung of the ladder. Above my head, the duck-billed conductor is waiting on top of the podium, ready to start the band. "I'll get the platypus."

As I climb the ladder, I can't stop myself from grinning. For the first time since I got here, I'm in control. My head's buzzing with excitement. I'm going to steal an antique platypus, and I don't even care if I get caught.

When Mum first got ill, I tried so hard to do the right thing all the time, not wanting to cause her any worry or make things worse. But even though I kept everything bottled up inside—the bullying at school, my dad's disappearing acts—this didn't help make Mum any better, and I just had to watch her fade away. But in this universe, there's no Mum for me to worry about anymore. Here, I can do what I like—just like Bad Albie does.

From the top of the ladder, the platypus seems a bit farther away than it looked from the floor, but it looks twice as freaky. On top of the white tuxedo, a black bow tie is knotted beneath its enormous beak, and its beady eyes stare back at me suspiciously.

"Have you got it?" Wesley calls out.

Holding on to the ladder with one hand, I reach out for the platypus. It's about as big as my backpack, with a couple of nasty-looking spikes near the front of its flippers. My mouth is dry and I can feel my heart thudding in my chest as I grab hold of its shiny brown fur. And that's when everything starts to go wrong.

"I can't wait to see the animals!" It's Miss Benjamin's voice, and it sounds like she's right outside. "I used to love bringing the children to see them in the old museum. Thank you for giving me this sneak peek."

Panicking, I glance toward the frosted doors and see two shadows behind the glass. Miss Benjamin is going to catch me red-handed.

"What do we do now?" I hiss, but when I look down, Wesley has already let go of the bottom of the ladder and is heading toward a sign that says EMERGENCY EXIT. I'm on my own.

Then several things happen at once.

Without Wesley holding on, the ladder starts to jolt backward, tipping me forward into empty air. One second I'm reaching out for the platypus, and the next it's the only thing I'm holding on to as I fall toward the platform. On the way down, my flailing elbow somehow connects with a button on the side of the podium, switching it from Off to On.

As the runaway ladder picks up speed, trundling down the walkway toward the cricketing crocodiles and kangaroos, the sound of an orchestra suddenly fills the room. A fanfare of trumpets announces my arrival as I crash-land in the middle of the animal orchestra, a row of flute-playing huskies cushioning my fall.

As I lie there dazed, a stuffed penguin stabbing me in the ribs with its violin bow, I hear a huge crash as the ladder smashes into the platform at the bottom of the walkway. I'm still holding on to the platypus, and when I open my eyes, its beak is millimeters away from my face and its beady gaze tells me I've made a massive mistake.

I scramble to my feet, and the orchestra is still blaring, but the stuffed musicians are scattered across the stage. My crash landing has taken out the brass and woodwind sections, and most of the penguin violinists too. On the other side of the room, the kangaroos' cricket match has been completely demolished, and one of the crocodile batsmen is now stuck halfway up the ladder. Wesley is nowhere to be seen.

"Albie Bright!" Miss Benjamin shrieks. With a sinking feeling, I turn to see my prematurely aged teacher standing in the doorway, her left eye now twitching into hyperdrive. Next to her, the museum curator is shaking his head in horror as he surveys the devastation. "What on earth have you done?"

ON THE TV, DOC BROWN IS HANGING FROM THE clock tower as Marty McFly accelerates the DeLorean to eighty-eight miles per hour, ready to take the time machine back to the future. It's weird—I must have seen this film at least fifty times, but even though the story is exactly the same, the Marty McFly in this movie looks completely different. I guess some other actor must have played the part in this parallel universe. But I'm not really watching the film—I'm just sitting on the living room sofa, waiting for Granddad Joe to start talking to me.

He hasn't said a word since he turned up at the museum to take me home, listening in silence as Miss Benjamin angrily listed my "crimes":

Destruction of an animatronic animal orchestra
Demolition of the kangaroos versus crocodiles cricket match
Attempted theft of an antique stuffed platypus

Even when Miss Benjamin told Granddad Joe that I was suspended from school for a week pending further inquiries, he didn't say a word. Instead we walked back home together in silence and he sat down in his armchair with a heavy sigh, turning on the TV that was still showing the same film I'd last seen in another universe.

I shouldn't care about any of this. I can just climb back inside my cardboard box and leave this mess for Bad Albie to sort out. After all, none of this would have happened if he hadn't forced me to go to school instead of him. But then I see the look of disappointment on Granddad Joe's face, and I can't help feeling that I've let him down.

"Granddad?" I say, desperately wishing he'd talk to me.

But he just sits in his armchair, staring at the TV as the lightning hits the clock tower.

"Granddad?" I say again, a bit louder this time in case his hearing aid's switched off.

Granddad Joe sighs in reply. "I can't even look at you, Albie," he says as the DeLorean disappears in a flash of electricity. "Not after what you've done this time."

"But I didn't mean to—"

"I used to take your mum to that museum when she

was a little girl," he tells me. "Of course, it wasn't called Fusion then—it was the Clackthorpe Museum of Natural History and Mechanical Wonders. Charlotte used to love looking at all the animals. She'd keep asking me questions. How high can a kangaroo hop? What's the difference between a turtle and a tortoise? Why is it that every animal is different? Your mum told me once that it was looking at the animals in the museum that made her want to be a scientist when she grew up. And I've just had to listen to your teacher telling me that you've destroyed half of these creatures with your stupid prank."

Shaking his head, Granddad Joe rubs his eyes, trying to hide the sadness that's started to leak out.

"What do you think your mum would say?"

This makes me feel like I've just been punched in the stomach. Of all the things Granddad Joe could say to me, this is the absolute worst. Everything I've done has been for my mum—inventing the Quantum Banana Theory, risking my life to kidnap a psychopathic cat, traveling to a parallel universe—but how can I explain any of this to Granddad Joe? There's only one thing I can say.

"I'm sorry, Granddad."

"Are you?" he asks doubtfully, looking at me for the first time. "That's what you always say. Look, Albie, I know your dad's not around much at the moment—rushing back and forth with his cold fusion thingamajigs—but that's no excuse for the way you're behaving. I know you think I'm a silly old man who can't even cook dinner without burning it, but your dad is trying to make the world a better place for you to grow up in." I can see the tears in Granddad Joe's eyes as he stares into mine. "When I look at you, Albie, I can see my Charlotte too. You're the spitting image of your mum. She also wanted to make the world a better place, and now it's up to you to make her proud."

I nod, fighting back my own tears. *Make her proud . . .* that's all I ever wanted to do.

"Don't worry, Granddad," I tell him, trying to keep my emotions in check as I get up off the sofa. "I'm going to put things right."

As I climb the stairs up to the attic, a guilty feeling follows me. Everything Granddad Joe said is whirring around my head, but I can't face up to it now. All I want to do is get out of this place. Part of me feels like I'm running away, but if I'm going to put things right, then I need to find my mum. My bedroom door is open, and as I step inside, it looks like the coast is clear.

The cardboard box is waiting for me in the corner of the room—my ticket out of this parallel universe. I only hope that it's not a one-way ticket. What if the Quantum Banana Theory doesn't work again? I try to push this nagging worry to the back of my mind.

Kneeling down, I check that everything is in the right

place. The Geiger counter is still hooked up to my mum's laptop, the banana in front of it now covered in brown splotches. It looks like I'm ready to go.

"What do you think you're doing?"

At the sound of my own voice, I spin around to see Bad Albie standing in the doorway, a cartoon scowl scrawled across his face.

"I sent you to school to keep everyone off my back, but you've just made things a thousand times worse. You've wrecked the museum and got me suspended from school, and when Dad finds out he's going to ground me forever. What's the big idea? I thought you clones were supposed to do what you're told."

He glares at me as if daring me to disagree.

"I told you before," I snap back at him. "I'm not a clone. I'm you—from a parallel universe."

Bad Albie just looks at me like I'm a moron.

"A parallel what?"

But I don't get the chance to answer his question, because a ginger streak of fur rockets into the room.

"What the—"

With a meow that sounds like a panther with a hangover, Dylan darts past Bad Albie and dives inside the cardboard box, its flaps falling shut behind him. For a second we both stand there in stunned silence; then I hear the clicking sound of the Geiger counter inside.

No! Not without me!

"Was that a cat?" Bad Albie asks, looking kind of worried as he walks toward the box. He grabs hold of the gardening gloves that I wore when I first arrived here, picking them up off the floor. "We've got to get it out of that box before it thinks it's kitty litter time and stinks up my room."

He shoves the gloves into my hands.

"Get ready to grab it when I open the flaps."

Leaning forward, Bad Albie slowly opens the box, waiting for the cat to spring out.

Nothing happens.

With a puzzled look on his face, he peers inside to find a banana, a Geiger counter, and my mum's laptop. There is no cat. Dylan has done it again.

Scratching his head, Bad Albie turns back to look at me in confusion.

"Where's the cat gone?"

So I tell him about the Quantum Banana Theory.

When I finish explaining everything, Bad Albie is still scratching his head.

"So you're telling me that my next-door neighbor's cat is now in a parallel universe?"

"No, Dylan's *my* next-door neighbor's cat," I correct him.

"And you're from a parallel universe too?"

"Yes, that's what I told you."

A huge grin lights up my evil twin's face.

"This is brilliant."

This is when I find out that the one thing worse than a parallel-universe Albie who doesn't believe me is one who does.

"So if I climb inside this box, I'll travel to a parallel universe?" he asks, peering at Mum's laptop as a stream of zeroes and ones pulses across the screen.

"Yes, but you see, the important thing is we can find Mum and—"

Bad Albie shakes his head.

"I don't care about my mum. I never even knew her. No, if this magic box can take me to another world, I'm going to find the one where my stupid dad hasn't given all his money away to charity." He narrows his eyes as he stares back at me. "I should be a millionaire—and in a parallel universe I will be."

For a second I'm lost for words. How can he say he doesn't care about Mum? She's the reason I invented the Quantum Banana Theory. The only thing that matters is finding her again.

"Come on," Bad Albie growls. "What do I need to do to get this thing working?"

If I let Bad Albie climb inside that box, he'll wreck everything. I've got to think of a way to stop him.

I'm still holding the gardening gloves, and as I glance down at them, a crazy idea jumps into my mind. I just need to convince this other Albie that it's true.

"If you want to travel to a parallel universe, then you've got to wear the right gear," I tell him, throwing the gloves straight back at him. "Just like I did."

Catching hold of them, Bad Albie looks at me like I've just told him to wear a tutu.

"A pair of gardening gloves?"

He couldn't sound more suspicious, but if this plan's going to work, I've got to convince him.

"Not just the gloves," I say. "You need to wear the mask and the body armor too. You don't want your insides turned into spaghetti when you go through the black hole into a parallel universe, do you? The body armor will keep all your bits in place, and the mask will protect your face from the cosmic rays."

Bad Albie looks down at the scary clown Halloween mask and my BMX body armor, which are still lying on the floor where I left them.

"Are you sure?" he asks doubtfully.

"It got me here in one piece, didn't it?" I pick up the protective vest and push it into his hands. "But if you want to risk your insides being squeezed out of your eyes like toothpaste from a tube, you go right ahead."

Still grumbling, Bad Albie starts to pull the chest armor on.

This is my only chance. While he's trying to pull the BMX vest that is too small over his head, I'm crawling inside the cardboard box. Trying not to make a noise, I pull the cardboard flaps shut behind me, fumbling in the dark to find the Geiger counter.

I look down at the readout, but there's no light coming from the display. It's dead. On the laptop screen, the zeroes and ones are still scrolling so quickly that they blur into one. But something's gone wrong. There's no power reaching the Geiger counter. If the banana goes radioactive, then how am I going to know if the universe has split in two?

Scrabbling in the darkness, I feel for the cable that connects the Geiger counter to the laptop, and my fingers brush against the end of the USB connector. Somehow Dylan must've disconnected it.

"Hey, where have you gone?"

I hear my own voice from outside the box, and I don't sound very happy.

With a shaking hand, I jab the connector into the USB port of Mum's laptop. With my other hand I grab hold of the banana, holding it next to the Geiger counter as I mutter under my breath in desperation.

"Come on, come on, come on."

The side of the cardboard box bulges as Bad Albie aims a kick at it.

"You—"

Then I hear the Geiger counter click, and the world seems to freeze for a millisecond. I feel a billion invisible elastic bands twang somewhere outside the box, and then the Geiger counter clicks again and my evil twin's shout snaps into silence.

Crouching there in the darkness, I try to catch my breath. It looks like the Quantum Banana Theory has worked again. The only thing I want to know is: where am I now?

THIS TIME I'VE LEARNED MY LESSON. OPENING the flaps, I cautiously peek my head out of the box, keeping my fingers crossed that I don't get punched in the face.

My bedroom looks exactly the same. There's my telescope and piles of books and comics; even the poster of the solar system is on the wall above my bed. I do a quick count of the planets—Mercury, Venus, Earth, Mars, Jupiter, Saturn, Uranus, Neptune—and breathe a sigh of relief that there are only eight this time.

It's only when I climb out of the box that I realize there's someone sitting at my desk. The person's back is to me, but I can tell at once it's me—I mean, another me.

"I can't believe you're here."

This other Albie turns around, and my jaw drops to

the floor as I see a girl staring back at me. It's like looking into a funfair mirror. Her face looks the same as mine—eyes, nose, and mouth all the same shape and in the same place—but she's definitely a girl.

I open and close my mouth a few times, but no words come out.

I suppose I shouldn't be so surprised. Every cell in your body contains chromosomes that make you who you are. What color eyes you have, how tall you are, whether or not you're going to need glasses. All this information is in your chromosomes. There's even a special pair of chromosomes that decide whether you're a boy or a girl. If you get an X and a Y chromosome, you're a boy, but if you get two Xs, then you're a girl. It's a fifty-fifty chance. The Albie in this universe must have got two Xs.

While I'm still doing an impression of a drowning goldfish, this Girl Albie is looking back at me with the same shocked expression on her face.

"You're a boy," she says, shaking her head in disbelief.

What am I supposed to say? In the last parallel universe, the other Albie thought I was a clone, but there's no way I can pretend that now.

"I'm—"

"I know exactly who you are," Girl Albie replies, her words bubbling out in a torrent of excitement. "You're me from a parallel universe. Inside that cardboard box is a banana, a Geiger counter, and Mum's quantum computer, which is hooked up to the Grid at CERN. Her experiments at the Large Hadron Collider have created a mini black hole that leads to a parallel universe. You've used the mini particle accelerator in Mum's quantum computer to replicate this, creating a wormhole through the fifth dimension that lets you travel to these parallel worlds. It's simple really. The Quantum Banana Theory works." She pauses for a second to catch her breath, a grin spreading across her lips. "I should know—I thought of it too."

My jaw drops open again. The Albie in this universe isn't just a girl, she's a genius as well. We both might have invented the Quantum Banana Theory, but to be honest, I haven't got a clue how it works. But Girl Albie seems to have it all worked out.

"I'm Alba, by the way," she tells me.

This time I manage to stutter out my own name in reply.

"I'm Albie."

Alba laughs.

"That figures," she says. "After Albert Einstein, right? Mum and Dad were never that creative when it came to names. Dad even called my pet hamster Hawking after the famous scientist."

I hear a familiar squeak from the desk behind her and catch a glimpse of Hawking scurrying around his wheel.

"Me too!" I tell her excitedly.

For a second we just grin at each other. In this parallel

universe I might have turned into a girl, but at least my hamster is still alive. But there's one thing I can't figure out.

"If you know all about the Quantum Banana Theory, then why haven't you tried it yourself?" I ask Alba. "You could have traveled to a parallel universe too."

Alba pushes her chair back from the desk, and I notice for the first time that it has wheels instead of legs.

"Since I ended up in this, I haven't felt like risking the trip," she tells me, the grin on her face slowly fading away.

I can't stop myself from staring at her wheelchair.

"What happened?"

"It was a car accident," Alba replies. "Mum was driving us to the airport to meet Dad, who was coming back from a filming trip. It was a foggy morning and there was a crash on the motorway—a drunk man driving a white van on the wrong side of the road. He smashed straight into us. I don't remember much after that. The car was a complete wreck, and Dad told me it took the firefighters three hours to cut us out." A tear starts to creep out of the corner of her eye. "I was lucky—I was just paralyzed from the waist down, but Mum didn't make it."

My brain is flashing up an error message, unable to make sense of what Alba's just told me. This can't be right. I've found my way to another parallel universe, but it's another world without my mum.

"What about your universe?" Alba asks me, rubbing

her eyes with the corner of her sleeve. "You can still walk. Did Mum survive the accident there?"

Still dazed, I shake my head, almost feeling guilty that I can walk and Alba can't.

"There was no car accident," I tell her.

"So Mum's still alive in your universe?" she asks eagerly. I recognize the spark of hope that suddenly lights up her eyes.

I shake my head again, not wanting to say the words out loud. This only makes them feel more real.

"No," I finally force myself to reply. "She died of cancer two weeks ago."

Alba's face crumples again, the tears in her eyes a mirror image of my own. I feel like we've both been cheated. Why can't there be a universe where Mum's still alive? We stare at each other, sharing our sadness in silence. Then the sound of Granddad Joe's voice comes up the stairs.

"Are you ready yet?"

Alba and I reply simultaneously, "I'm coming!"

The sound of our voices calling out together creates a weird echo, and I clap my hand over my mouth when I realize what I've done. Then I hear the sound of Granddad Joe's footsteps coming up the stairs.

"Have you got a boy up there, Alba?"

Alba looks at me, her eyes now wide with panic.

"Hide," she hisses.

I look around the room. It's just as messy as mine.

There's only one place I can hide—the same spot that got me here in the first place. As Granddad Joe opens the door, I dive inside the cardboard box.

"I thought I heard a boy's voice."

Granddad Joe sounds puzzled, like he's trying to work out how Alba replied to him in stereo. Luckily Alba's already thought up an explanation.

"I was just singing along to the radio while I was getting ready, Granddad."

I stay quiet inside the cardboard box. The banana is only centimeters away from my face, the light from the laptop screen making it glow green. Silently I pull out the USB cable, frightened that the click of the Geiger counter might give me away.

"He didn't sound like much of a singer to me," Granddad Joe sniffed. "You should listen to some proper music, like Bob Dylan. Now, that was a singer."

I wince, remembering when Granddad Joe drove me to the hospital to see Mum with *Bob Dylan's Greatest Hits* playing on the car stereo. I'd never heard of Bob Dylan before, but I think he must have been named after Dylan the cat—at least, that's what he sang like.

"Anyway, you need to get a move on, Alba, if you want me to take you to the party. It's nearly eight o'clock." Granddad Joe pauses for a second. "Have you been crying?" he asks.

"It's just hay fever," Alba replies quickly, and I hear her

blow her nose. "I'll be down in a second, Granddad. I've just got to finish getting ready."

"OK, but you need to be quick. The party started at seven, didn't it? And when you get back, we can talk about you tidying up this room."

I hear the bedroom door close, followed by the sound of footsteps heading downstairs. Then Alba lifts up the flap of the box, twisting her head at a ninety-degree angle to peer inside.

"I've got to go," she whispers, keeping her voice low in case Granddad Joe's got his hearing aid switched on. "It's Victoria Barnes's birthday party at the village hall tonight. Granddad's dropping me off and I've got a ride home for us, but you need to come and meet me there. I've got so much to tell you. If the Quantum Banana Theory really works, I think I know what you need to do to find Mum again."

"Alba!" yells Granddad Joe.

With a small, hopeful smile, Alba drops the cardboard flap, and then I hear her wheel her chair toward the door.

Inside the box, a blur of zeroes and ones are still flashing across the laptop screen, the data from the Large Hadron Collider somehow still streaming into the computer from across the universe. I hold the Geiger counter in my hand. If I plug it in, any moment now a radioactive particle in the banana is bound to decay, and the Quantum

Banana Theory will send me to another parallel universe. And maybe this one will have my mum in it.

Outside the bedroom door I hear a loud beep, followed by a whirring noise that sounds like an elevator going down. At first I can't work out what it is, and then I remember. If Alba's in a wheelchair, she must have a stairlift to help her get up and down the stairs.

I shake my head. It's just not fair. We've both lost Mum, but at least I can still walk.

Leaving the Geiger counter unplugged, I crawl out of the box. Alba said she knew what I needed to do to find Mum again. I'm not going to run away to another parallel universe without giving her the chance to tell me what it is.

I hear the front door slam shut downstairs. Alba is on her way to Victoria Barnes's birthday party, and I'm going to meet her there.

I can hear the party even before I get to the village hall, the thud of a song playing at full blast rumbling down the street. I recognize the song straightaway even though the words are all wrong.

Tiny changes—that's what my dad's book said I'd find in every parallel universe. Even in a song I've heard a thousand times before.

Outside the village hall, there are more balloons hung

up than even Buzz Lightyear would need to make it into orbit, and through the window I can see a tsunami of colored lights spinning across the ceiling.

"Albie!" Alba calls out to me from the door, pulling her wheelchair around in a nifty three-point turn. "You made it." She smiles.

It's kind of strange seeing her again. This time I'm noticing all the things that make her a girl. Her hair's a bit longer than mine to start with; her eyelashes are thicker; and even though our eyes, nose, and mouth all look pretty much the same, there's still some tiny differences that make Alba look like a girl and me a boy. We look the same, but different. Not an identical twin, but a sister, maybe, if I'd ever had one.

"We've got to go in right now," Alba says, looking a little bit stressed. "Victoria's going nuts because some people haven't turned up. She's two couples down for her dance competition."

I thought Alba just wanted to meet me here. I didn't think I'd actually have to go to Victoria Barnes's birthday party. Can't we just go and sit in the bus shelter, and Alba can tell me what I need to know?

Alba notices the sudden panic in my eyes.

"Don't worry," she says. "I've asked Victoria's mum if I can bring my cousin to the party, and she's says it's OK."

"Your cousin?"

"Well, I couldn't exactly say to her, 'Can I bring another Alba from a parallel universe?', could I?" she replies sarcastically. "'Oh, and by the way, he's a boy.'"

When she puts it like that, I kind of see her point.

As a new song booms out through the open door, I follow Alba inside the hall, only to find my worst nightmare waiting for me there.

MY SCHOOL REPORT SAYS I'VE GOT TWO LEFT feet. When we did traditional dances from history in PE, the rest of Class 6 all danced the waltz, the jive, the two-step, and the tango, but Miss Benjamin told me that I had to stick to the birdie dance. She said this was the best dance for a beginner like me, but I couldn't even get that right and ended up elbowing Timothy Chase in the face when I was trying to flap my wings in time. I forged a sick note from Granddad Joe to get me out of PE after that, but I still have nightmares in which Miss Benjamin is forcing me to dance the fox-trot.

So when I step into the village hall to see an enormous dance floor with hundreds of flashing lights and a huge glitterball hanging overhead, it's my worst nightmare come to life. On the dance floor, Wesley MacNamara is dancing with Victoria Barnes, the two of them cha-cha-cha-ing to a song that sounds kind of familiar but not quite right. Victoria's wearing a sparkly red dress that seems to be made entirely out of sequins, while Wesley is wearing an all-in-one white jumpsuit, although it looks like he's forgotten to button up his shirt.

As Wesley spins Victoria around for the final time, she finishes the song by doing the splits in the middle of the dance floor. The rest of Class 6, who are standing around the edge watching, break into a chorus of whoops and cheers. Next to the DJ, the spotlight falls on a panel of three judges—Miss Benjamin; Victoria's mum; and the vicar, who's wearing a gold lamé suit—each of them holding up a scorecard with a large number nine on it.

"What a surprise," Alba mutters as she pushes her wheelchair toward the dance floor. "Victoria wins again."

"I hate dancing," I tell her. "There's no scientific reason why people should dance."

"I used to like it," Alba replies, and I instantly feel like the stupidest person in the room. "Mum said to me that the atoms in our bodies are dancing all the time, so it's only fair that we play them some music to dance along to. Before the accident we used to dance around the kitchen together inventing routines for some of Mum's favorite songs."

I remember dancing around the kitchen too, but that just reminds me why I've come here.

I'm looking around for a quiet corner where I can ask Alba exactly what she meant when she said she knew what I needed to do to see Mum again, when I spot a familiar face. It's Kiran, standing waiting outside the party's inflatable photo booth. For a second I forget that the Kiran in this universe doesn't even know me, and I give him a friendly wave.

Kiran just stares straight past me like I'm the Invisible Man. Then he spots Alba, and I see the shy smile that appears on Kiran's face every time a girl he likes walks into the room. He gives her a wave, and looking across I watch Alba wave back, wearing the same shy smile. I can't stop myself from smiling too. At least the Albie in this universe has got the same best friend as me. Then a horrible thought creeps into my head—the question almost too terrifying to ask.

"Is Kiran your boyfriend?"

Alba turns a bright shade of beet.

"He's just a friend," she says quickly. "I mean, he did ask if I wanted to go and see *Back to the Future IV* at the cinema next week, but there's a whole gang of us going along." Alba looks up at me hopefully. "Do you think that means he likes me?"

Before this conversation can get any more embarrassing, Victoria Barnes arrives on the scene in a shimmy of red sequins, followed by Olivia, Kim, and the rest of her usual entourage. Just like Kiran, she stares straight past me, fixing her gaze on Alba instead.

"Albs," she says, a fake smile plastered to her face. "So nice of you to make it here at last."

"Sorry, Victoria," Alba replies, sounding more nervous than I've heard her before. "Something came up at home, and I couldn't get away."

"And who's this?" Victoria asks, finally turning her attention to me. "Your date?"

The last time I saw Victoria Barnes, she gave me a kiss in a parallel universe, but now she's looking at me like I've just crawled out from under a stone.

"No, this is my cousin, erm—Albie," Alba replies quickly. "He's staying with me for the weekend. Your mum said it was OK for me to bring him along to the party."

Victoria looks me up and down, her shimmering lips turning from a sneer into a smirk.

"Nice outfit for a party, lamebrain."

That's when I realize I'm still wearing my school uniform.

Olivia, Kim, and the rest of Victoria's posse start to giggle as my face turns the same shade of beet as Alba's. To be honest, I think I preferred the Victoria Barnes in the last universe.

"Anyway, Albs," Victoria says, grabbing hold of the armrest of Alba's wheelchair and twisting it so it faces her properly. "It's your turn to bust some moves on the dance floor. Everyone else has, and the judges are waiting."

I see a look of panic dart across Alba's face.

"You can't be serious," she replies, her voice cracking a little. "How am I supposed to dance in this?"

Alba gestures down at the wheelchair she's sitting in. From the look on her face I can see she's on the verge of tears, biting her lip in the same way I do whenever things get to be too much. Then I look back at Victoria, unable to believe she could be so mean.

"Don't be such a wuss, Alba," Victoria tuts, waving Alba's protest away in a shower of sequins. "Everyone else at my party has, and you're the one who's always going on about equality."

The music has gone quiet now, and most of Class 6 are watching Victoria, waiting to see what happens next.

"Anyway," she says, pointing her finger toward the borrowed Junior Dance Star leaderboard, her own name at the top with twenty-seven points. "Nobody expects you to win."

Alba glares up at Victoria. If her reddened eyes were laser beams, Victoria would be toast right now.

"But I haven't got anyone to dance with."

Victoria turns to point at me.

"How about lamebrain here? Let's face it, Alba, your cousin is probably the only person who'd want to dance with you anyway."

Alba bites her lip so hard that it almost turns white, and I feel a flash of anger rising in my chest. Victoria has gone too far. I might have two left feet. I might be wearing my school uniform. But there's no way I'm going to let her bully Alba and me in this parallel universe.

"I'd prefer to dance with Alba over you any day," I tell Victoria, loud enough so the rest of Class 6 can hear. "That dress makes you look like a tomato."

This gets a laugh from everyone, and even Olivia and Kim can't stop themselves from giggling. Before Victoria has the chance to reply, I hold out my hand to Alba.

"Let's show her how it's done."

Alba looks at me like I've just told her we're flying a spaceship to Mars. But she follows me anyway, wheeling her high-tech chair one-handed as we head across the dance floor to where the DJ is waiting.

"What are you doing?" she hisses, keeping her voice low. "You already told me you think dancing is stupid. Now you want me to start twerking in this stupid wheelchair. Everyone's going to laugh at me."

I shake my head. I've got a plan. I might not be great at traditional dances from history, but there's a few dance steps that I still remember. I only hope that in this universe, Alba remembers them too.

"You said you used to dance around the kitchen with Mum. Did she ever show you her old-school hip-hop moves?"

Looking puzzled, Alba nods. "The ones for that 'Intergalactic' song? I laughed so much I nearly choked on my pizza." Then she stares at me with her eyes open wide. "Oh no, you can't be serious."

With a nod from the DJ, Alba and I take our positions in the middle of the dance floor. Around the edges, the rest of Class 6 is looking on—waiting to see how stupid we make ourselves look. Alba's in her wheelchair to the right of me, her arms folded across her chest, while I've borrowed a baseball cap and put it on backward to give my school uniform more of a hip-hop flavor. If everyone's going to laugh, I might as well give them something to laugh about.

Then the sample of a droning robotic voice kicks in, and I'm already moving in time to the beat as the song blares out.

Keeping my arms bent at ninety-degree angles, I swivel to the right, moving one muscle at a time as I jerk my arms in a stop-start rhythm before snapping my head in the same direction. I see Alba doing the same, both of us dancing like robots from the year 3000 as the intergalactic chorus of the song rings out again.

I push one shoulder up to my ear, tilt, and straighten from right to left and back again. A robotic wave rolls through our bodies as we pop, lock, and drop in perfect symmetry. In the front of the watching crowd, I see Victoria mutter something to Kim, who just giggles in reply.

I couldn't look any more stupid, but I just don't care, my arms jerking in time with the dancing molecules in the air as the song fills the room.

As the DJ scratches, Alba and I drop straight into a frozen dance pose. One hand on the hip, the other pointing to the sky as the rappers babble out their lyrics in time with the techno beat. With each chorused line we switch position, arms folded in a hip-hop pose, then throwing out Tetris shapes as the robotic voice kicks in again.

Inside my head, I can see Mum voguing around the kitchen with a massive grin on her face. I remember calling out the names of different shapes—square, rhombus, triangle—as she switched from one frozen pose to the next.

I hear a cheer from the crowd as I drop straight back into the robot dance. My arms jerk from side to side, stuttering to a halt and then speeding up again. Next to me, Alba does the same as we swivel around to face each other. Somehow, even though we're dancing, we can't stop ourselves from grinning, and the smile on Alba's face matches my own as we move to the beat.

Around the edge of the dance floor, the rest of Class 6 starts to join in. I can see Wesley MacNamara jerking robotically in his white jumpsuit, and even Olivia and Kim are now bobbing their heads in time with the tune. Only Victoria is standing still, her eyes turned to laser beams aiming death rays in my direction.

My arms raised, I point to the stars as Alba does the

same, bouncing on the spot just like Mum did as the robotic voice calls out the chorus to the rest of the class.

Now everybody's doing the same, and the dance floor is bouncing as we're surrounded. Nobody cares how stupid they look. Alba and I are lost in the crowd as every corner of the room rocks to the robotic beat.

I realize now why people dance. You don't feel alone when you're lost in a song. Closing my eyes for a second, I catch another glimpse of my mum in my mind—a smile on her face as she watches me dance. But when I open them again, she's gone.

As the song ends in a fanfare of scratches, everyone is cheering, and it's only when I look toward the spotlight now shining on the panel of judges that I see the reason why. The judges are all holding their scorecards in the air—each one giving Alba and me a perfect ten.

"THANKS."

Alba turns back to smile at me as she reaches the top of the stairs.

"What for?"

Lifting the guardrail, Alba wheels her chair off the stairlift.

"That was the first time I've danced since the accident," she replies. "Since Mum died. I'd forgotten how much fun it can be."

Alba nudges my—I mean her—bedroom door open, wheeling herself forward as I follow close behind. Granddad Joe was snoring in his armchair when we got back home, *Back to the Future* on the TV as we sneaked past the living room door. Now it was time for me to find out what

Alba really meant when she said she knew what I had to do to find Mum again.

"Do you still miss her?" I ask.

"Every day," she replies. Alba glances up at the square of stars shining through the skylight. "Sometimes I sit here in the dark, looking through my telescope at the stars, and I remember all the things she told me. It makes me feel like she's still here with me now."

I think about how close I am to finding Mum again, and a tingle of excitement runs down my spine. Then Alba clicks the light switch on, and we both see that something is very wrong.

The telescope is still there pointing out the skylight, but the piles of books and comics have all been tidied away, and in the middle of the room there's no sign at all of my cardboard box.

"What's happened?" I ask, instantly starting to panic. "Where's the box?"

Alba is holding her head in her hands.

"Granddad Joe must have tidied my room."

Inside the shed the cardboard box is lying on its side, half crushed beneath a pile of recycling. Next to it is a green caddy filled with food waste, a browning banana sticking out of the top. And at the back of the shed, I can see Mum's quantum computer shoved out of the way on the workbench with the Geiger counter lying on top. It looks like it's ready to be dismantled as it sits there surrounded by the rest of Dad's abandoned projects and DIY jobs.

I walk over to the laptop and press the power button, but the screen stays blank. The battery must have run flat—just like any hope I had that I'd see Mum again.

"I'm sorry," Alba says, wheeling her chair to the workbench. "I didn't realize that Granddad Joe would start tidying my room without me. When he saw the cardboard box, he must've just thought it was some of Dad's old stuff—ready for recycling."

I don't say anything back. The Quantum Banana Theory was the one chance I had of finding a parallel universe where Mum was still alive. With the experiment ruined, I'm stranded here. No chance of finding Mum. No way back home.

Alba looks up at me. In the dim light of the shed, I see my own eyes staring back, a glint of determination in her gaze.

"We can fix this," she says. "And while we do, I'll tell you how quantum physics can help you find Mum."

With the laptop plugged into the charger and the banana rescued from the recycling, Alba starts to explain what she means.

"Atoms and particles can behave in really strange ways—"

"I know all this," I snap, struggling to straighten out

the caved-in sides of my cardboard box. One corner of the box feels a bit damp and smells funny, like a cat's peed in it. "Sometimes the same particle can be in two places at once—that's how scientists knew that parallel universes could exist."

Frowning, Alba gives me the same look Dad does whenever a TV interviewer interrupts him to ask a really stupid question.

"That's not what I was going to tell you," she replies with a scowl.

As Alba is currently sitting next to some heavy-duty tools, including a claw hammer and a particularly lethal-looking pair of pliers, I quickly shut my mouth and let her get on with the explanation.

"The weirdest thing about quantum physics," she says, "isn't that the same particle can be in two places at the same time, but that two different particles can act like they're the same particle."

"What's so special about that?"

"Scientists call it quantum entanglement," Alba explains. "It's when two particles are joined together in a strange and peculiar way. Anything you discover about one of the particles instantly becomes true for the other particle too, no matter where it is. You can take these two particles to opposite ends of the universe, but they stay connected. If you find out that one of the particles is spinning, then this means that the other particle will be spinning in exactly the same way—even though it's on the other side of the universe. It's like there's some sort of telepathic link between the entangled particles that lets them communicate faster than the speed of light."

I can't stop myself from interrupting Alba again.

"That's impossible," I tell her, remembering a fact I learned from one of my dad's TV programs. "Albert Einstein said that nothing can travel faster than the speed of light—not even weird mind-reading particles that put each other in a spin. It's against the laws of science."

"Not according to quantum physics," Alba replies. "The particles share the same quantum state—even though they're billions of light-years apart. Albert Einstein called it 'spooky action at a distance' because he thought it was so impossibly weird, but scientists have carried out experiments that prove quantum entanglement really exists."

By the time Alba has got to the end of her explanation, I'm more confused than when she started. My brain hurts. Quantum physics is giving me a headache. It's time to cut to the chase.

"How's this going to help me find Mum?"

"Don't you see?" Alba says, sounding more like Dad by the minute. "If entangled particles can stay connected at opposite ends of the universe, then why not across parallel universes too?"

She picks up the pliers from the workbench, and for

a second I'm worried she's going to do some DIY on me for interrupting her again, but instead she waves them in the air.

"The particles in these pliers must be entangled with the particles in the same pair of pliers in another parallel universe. If you want to find the other pair, you just need to take a quantum look at these, and they'll tell you what you need to know. To find Mum, we need something that belonged just to her—something precious, like a ring or a necklace maybe. We'll be able to use this to find the parallel universe where she still has it. The world where she's still alive."

Inside my heart a tiny spark of hope flickers into life. Something precious that belonged just to Mum . . .

Digging deep inside my pocket, I pull out the ammonite that Mum and I found on the moors. Its golden spiral shape glints in the half-light as Alba gasps in recognition.

"Dad was going to make this into a necklace for Mum," I tell her, "but he never got around to it."

"He did in this universe," she says, reaching out to touch the fossil as if she can't quite believe it's real. "Mum used to wear the necklace every day. But after she died, Dad lost his temper and threw the necklace against the wall. He said it was too painful to see it lying around without Mum there to wear it. The ammonite smashed into a thousand pieces." Alba's fingers reach up to her neck, pulling out a gold chain from beneath her T-shirt. "This is all I've got left."

I stare at the necklace, a loop of wire dangling emptily from the chain. Then I look down at the 100-million-year-old fossil in the palm of my hand. Somehow it feels even more precious to me now.

"So what do we do?"

"First we use the ammonite from your universe to fix Mum's necklace," Alba says, holding out her hand for it.

Almost reluctantly, I hand it over. Alba takes the chain from around her neck and places it next to the fossil on the workbench. Then she uses the pliers to carefully twist the loop of wire around and around the ammonite, creating a nest to hold it in place. Such a simple thing to do, but somehow my dad never found the time.

Alba turns back toward me, the spiral fossil shimmering as it dangles from the necklace chain.

"It looks just like it used to," she murmurs. "The same necklace Mum wore every day."

It's stupid, but I can't help feeling a little bit jealous of Alba. In this parallel world, Dad found the time to make Mum the necklace—and cared enough about Mum to smash it into pieces when she was gone. What else have I missed out on? Maybe I was born in the wrong universe?

I take the necklace out of Alba's hand, staring at the ammonite as it spirals around. It's time to find the right one.

"So what do we do with it?"

Alba reaches up to the workbench to grab what looks like a thermos covered with wires, cables, and duct tape.

"We put it inside this."

"What's that?" I ask. To be honest, I'm not sure how putting a fossil inside a high-tech thermos of tea will help me find my mum.

"It's a quantum entangler," Alba replies. "I built it myself. It can calculate the quantum state of any particles that are put inside." She lifts up the dangling USB cable sticking out of the bottom of the thermos. "If we hook this up to Mum's quantum computer, then it should be able to pinpoint the exact parallel universe where the other necklace is located and, fingers crossed, you'll find Mum wearing it there."

I can't stop myself from grinning. If what Alba's saying is true, she's invented a quantum GPS that can take me straight to Mum. It might sound big-headed for me to say this, but this female version of me is seriously amazing.

"How did you end up such a brainbox?" I ask her.

"You're just as brainy as me," Alba says with a grin, our smiles a perfect match. "We both invented the Quantum Banana Theory, after all. All we need to do now is rebuild the experiment with the quantum entangler hooked up too. That should do the trick."

"What are we waiting for?" I say, desperate to find out if this really will work. "Let's get entangling!"

As we work together to set up the experiment, I start

to realize what it would be like to have a sister or brother. Because things were a bit tricky for me healthwise when I was born, Mum and Dad decided not to risk having another baby. I didn't mind. Mum was always there for me—inventing brilliant games, answering all my questions, making me feel like I was never alone.

As Alba unscrews the top of the thermos and places the necklace inside, I think about how fun it would be to have a sister—someone to hang out with, to talk to, to look out for when things go wrong. Someone who would share their quantum entangler with me.

Alba screws the lid back on top of the thermos. "Let's try it," she says, looking up at me excitedly.

I plug the quantum entangler's USB cable into Mum's laptop, using the spare port next to where the Geiger counter is hooked up. Then, with my heart thudding in my chest, I press the power button.

The laptop screen lights up instantly, and I see a stream of numbers blurring into one—an avalanche of data scrolling endlessly. I look back at Alba, her face lit up by the same glow.

"It works," she says, almost sounding like she can't believe it herself.

"But I still can't seem to wrap my head around just how," I say. "This data is coming from the Large Hadron Collider in *my* universe. How can the laptop still be connected to the Grid?"

"This is a quantum computer," Alba replies. "It works by using copies of itself in other parallel universes to crunch the data. That's what makes it so powerful. It's not just connected to the Grid in your universe, but every parallel universe—"

Alba's explanation is cut off by the sound of a voice outside.

"Alba, are you in there?"

It's Granddad Joe.

I exchange a panicked glance with Alba. It would be impossible to explain to Granddad Joe what we're doing in Dad's workshop. There's no time to talk and only one place to hide. Lifting the laptop from the workbench, I climb inside the rebuilt cardboard box as Alba stalls for time.

"Coming, Granddad!" she shouts. "I'm just sorting out the recycling."

As I crouch at the bottom of the box, trying to ignore the smell of cat pee, Alba hisses at me.

"Albie!"

Looking up, I see her holding out the banana she's rescued from the green caddy. Its yellow skin is almost completely covered with brown splotches, and it wouldn't win any fruit bowl beauty competition, but it's the missing piece I need for the experiment to work.

"Thanks," I say, reaching out to grab hold of it. I put the banana down next to the Geiger counter in the corner of the box. Then I look back up at Alba. "For everything."

"Good luck," she says, biting her bottom lip to stop her eyes from leaking.

I can feel my own eyes filling with tears. There's only time to ask her one last question.

"If I find Mum again, what should I do?"

Alba wipes her eyes with the back of her hand.

"Tell her that I love her," she says.

Then she closes the cardboard flaps over my head, leaving me alone in the dark.

The laptop screen is glowing green, the flashing zeroes and ones calculating the quantum state of the ammonite necklace inside the quantum entangler. Outside the box I hear the shed door open and the sound of Granddad Joe's voice. But before I have the chance to hear what he's saying, the Geiger counter clicks and the universe shivers into silence.

It's happened again.

Wiping a tear from my eye, I take a deep breath before I reach up to open the lid of the box. This time, will Mum be waiting for me outside?

I LIFT UP THE LID OF THE BOX, AND I KNOW straightaway that something is wrong. When I climbed into the box a few seconds ago in another universe, the only light came from a single lightbulb overhead, but now bright sunshine is flooding in through the shed window. It seems as if I've traveled forward in time as well, skipping from night to day in the switch from one universe to the next.

Feeling nervous, I climb out of the box, not sure what other differences I'm going to find in this new parallel world.

The shed door is open, and as I look around, I almost fall back into the box in shock when I see my dad sitting at the workbench. He's looking away from me, his head bent as he twists the loop of wire around the spiral ammonite, attaching this to the necklace chain. For a split second I think I'm back at home in my own universe, but then I realize that the fossil from my world is still inside the quantum entangler.

In my universe, Dad never got around to making this necklace, but it looks like I've found a universe where he did, and that must mean Mum's still alive.

"Albie!" Dad says, dropping the pliers in surprise as he glances up to see me. "I didn't even hear you come in." Then he shakes his head with a look of confusion on his face. "Weren't you supposed to get back tomorrow? I'd have picked you up from school if I'd known you were coming back early. Did you enjoy your school trip to London? How was the Natural History Museum?"

Here's more proof that this isn't my universe. I've never even been to the Natural History Museum.

Dad's still staring at me as he waits for an answer, so I blurt out the first word that comes into my head.

"Dinosaurs."

"Dino-what?" Dad says with a puzzled frown. "I don't think I've heard that word before. Is this something new you're doing at school?"

Feeling confused, I quickly change the subject.

"What are you doing in here?" I ask him. "Aren't you supposed to be working down in the mine today?"

Dad shakes his head.

"You know I'm only working three days a week now—

just like everyone else. There's not enough coal left down there for us to bring out much more." He looks down at the fossil he's holding, its trailing chain still left unfastened. "So I thought I'd get on with an unfinished project instead."

Now I'm seriously confused. Dad's talking like he's a coal miner, not a famous scientist. But the only thing that really matters to me is sitting in the palm of his hand.

"You're making Mum's necklace," I say.

Dad traces his finger around the spiral fossil, the ammonite sparkling gold in the sunlight.

"Yeah," he replies, nodding thoughtfully. "Better late than never, I thought."

I can't hide my excitement anymore.

"Can I see Mum when you give it to her?"

I see a flash of pain in Dad's eyes, but he quickly tries to hide this.

"Good idea," he says, forcing a smile onto his face. He fastens the clasp and then slips the necklace into his pocket. "It's been a while since we last went to see her together."

It's a sunny day, but I can't get rid of the cold in my bones as I stare down at the gravestone.

IN LOVING MEMORY OF
CHARLOTTE ELIZABETH BRIGHT

Dad hangs the necklace around the neck of the angel that's carved at the head of the stone. Another stupid universe where Mum is dead, and I don't even know why. Cancer. Car accident. I can't even bring myself to ask. I thought that this time it'd be different. I keep biting my lip, but I can't stop myself from crying anymore.

"It's OK," Dad says, putting his arm around my shoulder. "I still miss her too. I think that's why I wanted to finish the necklace for her—even after all these years. While I was making it, it let me forget—just for a while—that she wasn't still here."

He pulls a tissue out of his pocket and pushes it into my hand.

"It's not fair," I sniff, wiping my nose with a shudder.

"I know it's not fair," Dad says, "but as long as we stick together like she told us to, it'll be OK."

A cold wind whips in from the moor, cutting through the graveyard. I shiver as the shadow of St. Thomas's spire dips closer to the gravestone.

"When your mum died, I felt lost," Dad continues, his arm hugging me tight to protect me from the cold. "The only thing I could do was work every hour of every day and try to forget. That was when there was still enough coal to mine, of course. But you helped me face up to things, Albie. You made me see that life was still worth living—even without your mum."

Turning my head, I look up at Dad's face and see the tears shining in his eyes.

"Top of the class; brainy like your mum. She'd be so proud of you, Albie. Just like I am."

I don't know what to say. I'm not the Albie he thinks I am. But with his arm around my shoulder, for the moment I just don't care.

The wind's getting stronger now, whipping the heads of the flowers that Dad's laid on Mum's gravestone.

"There's a good wind getting up," he says, glancing out over the moor. "How about we head back to the workshop and make a start on that kite I've been promising you."

Back in the shed, Dad shows me how to make a kite. He gets two long, thin sticks, and I help him glue them together in the shape of a cross. Wrapping one piece of string around the middle for reinforcement, Dad threads another piece through the notches at the ends of the sticks to make a frame for the kite. Then we dig out old newspapers from the recycling and use these to cover up the frame.

I read some of the front-page headlines as we stick the newspapers down. ENERGY CRISIS. NO COAL NO GO. POWER CUTS STRIKE. It doesn't sound like things are going so well in this parallel world. Maybe this is what Dad was talking about when he said he was only working three days a week. But I don't have time to find out more now as Dad fixes a ball of string to the frame.

"I think it's ready," he says, holding up the newspaper kite. "Let's go up on the moor to give it a test flight."

Even as I'm carrying it up the hill, the wind is tugging at the kite, eager to set it free. While we're walking, Dad's asking me all sorts of questions about the school trip, my friends, and what I want to do for the rest of the weekend.

My head's spinning. I don't know what the Albie in this universe would say. He's still in London on a school trip with Class 6, and I feel like I'm just borrowing his dad for the day. But the thing is, deep down, I'm kind of starting to wish I could stay.

At the top of the hill I keep hold of the string, and Dad runs to launch the kite into the air. As soon as he lets it go, the kite soars into the sky like a newspaper plane. I quickly let out more string as it twists, turns, and tugs, the kite flying higher with each fresh gust of wind that sweeps across the moor. I can see St. Thomas's Church from here, Dad joining me to watch as the kite soars above the spire.

"Keep a tight hold, Albie," he says, lifting his hand to shield his eyes against the sun. "Never let her go."

And I think of Mum and how that's the one thing I won't ever do.

I sit in the kitchen watching Dad as he makes us cheese on toast.

I'm tired but happy. After flying the kite for an hour or two, we headed back to the workshop, where Dad decided we should build a life-size Transformer out of cardboard boxes, turning it from a car to a robot to a plane and back again. He even got out an old-fashioned camcorder, and we spent the rest of the afternoon making a movie as I pretended to rescue planet Earth from evil robot invaders.

Don't worry, I made sure that the cardboard box with the quantum banana experiment in it was kept safely out of the way. I asked Dad to help me take it up to my bedroom, telling him it was for a school project I was working on. He asked if he could help me with it, but I thought it would be a bit weird if I started explaining quantum physics to my dad.

But all the time we were together, we just kept on talking—Dad answering any question I asked, just like Mum used to. I've never had so much fun with him before. It's like he's had a personality transplant in this parallel universe and swapped brains with the dad out of that book Mrs. Forest gave me to read, *Danny the Champion of the World.*

Now, as the light outside the kitchen window fades, Dad shovels the cheese on toast onto two plates, Marmite melted in with the cheese on mine, just how I like it.

"You're a bit quiet, Albie," he says, carrying the plates over to the kitchen table. "What's on your mind?"

This is when I decide to stop worrying about what the Albie in this universe would say, and instead start to tell Dad everything. How Wesley MacNamara always punches me in exactly the same place on my arm so that it hurts a little bit more every time. How Victoria Barnes calls me lamebrain, and how my best friend Kiran wants to send the first of something into space but he doesn't know what to choose. And Dad just listens to me, asking questions now and then before saying something that makes everything seem all right as we eat our cheese on toast.

I'm just about to tell him how I'm actually an Albie from a parallel universe, how I've already met my evil twin as well as a female version of myself, and how I thought I could use quantum physics to find Mum again but I can't seem to get it right. But before I have the chance to speak, all the lights go out.

"IS IT A POWER CUT?" I ASK.

I can hear Dad scrabbling around in the kitchen drawer as he searches for something. Then I see the spark of a match.

"You should be used to the nighttime curfew by now, Albie," he replies, lighting a candle and carrying it over to the table. "With the coal running out, the government's still rationing the electricity supply. They might get to keep the power running for longer down in London, but up here, it's still lights out by nine every night. Whether you've finished your cheese on toast or not."

Dad puts the candle down on the table between us and picks up his last piece of toast. In the orange glow of the candlelight, I can see a worried frown on his face.

"Are you feeling all right, Albie?" he asks me. "You didn't get a bang on your head while you were away, did you?"

I shake my head, but inside I'm kicking myself. Since I first climbed inside the cardboard box, I haven't felt as at home as I do right now. I know that Mum's still gone in this universe, but somehow Dad's making up for it as best he can. But just by asking one wrong question I've almost given myself away. I need to clear my head before I say anything else that shows I don't belong here.

"I'm fine, Dad," I tell him quickly. "I could just do with some fresh air."

Dad looks out the window, the sky now almost completely black and starting to sparkle with stars.

"How about we take the telescope out?" he says, clearing the plates away. "The moons should be coming out soon."

As Dad sets the telescope up on the patio, I snuggle inside my—I mean, the Albie from this universe's—fleece, the wind still whipping in from the moor, scudding clouds across the sky and making me shiver.

Behind me, the house lies in darkness. No electricity now until tomorrow morning. I know I should keep my mouth shut, but all the headlines I've read and what Dad's said have put a tiny worm of worry that's growing inside my head.

"Dad," I say. "What will happen when the coal runs out?"

Dad looks up from the viewfinder on the telescope, his face half hidden in the shadows.

"I'll have to get another job," he jokes. "No point in going down in the mine if there's nothing left to dig out."

"But you're a scientist," I say.

"I wish," Dad laughs. "You're saying some funny things today, Albie. I'm a coal miner—just like your Granddad Joe was before he passed away."

The last few words of Dad's sentence hit me like an invisible punch in the gut. I'd wondered where Granddad Joe was in this parallel world, but hadn't found the way to ask the question yet. Gone, just like Mum, and the universe seems to shrink a little bit more.

I thought quantum physics would help me put things right, but it just seems to be taking the people I love away from me over and over again. I bite my bottom lip to stop myself crying.

"Don't worry, Albie," Dad says, seeing the look on my face. "The government will find a way to make sure everything's OK. Since the oil ran out a few years back, they've had teams of scientists looking for new sources of power. The coal will last for a few more years yet, and they're bound to have worked something out by then."

In another universe Dad has invented cold fusion—unlimited energy for free—but in this universe he's just left sitting in the dark.

"Look," Dad says, pointing up at the sky as his face is lit with a strange new light. "The moons have come out."

The clouds are starting to clear, and as I look up into the night sky, I can't believe my eyes. There are two full moons in the sky, hanging there side by side. I blink hard, thinking at first that I'm seeing double, but when I open my eyes again, they're both still there. The words of my dad's book echo in my mind. *One tiny change . . .*

"Two moons," I breathe.

"Same as always." Dad grins. "No need to act so surprised. Now, shall we see if we can spot where Armstrong and Gagarin landed on each one?"

Through the telescope Dad shows me the geography of Moon One and Moon Two. He points out the Sea of Tranquility and the Ocean of Storms, the Apennine Mountains and the Fra Mauro crater, where Dad says the Apollo 13 mission landed. The plains, valleys, craters, and mountains on Moon One all look so familiar to me. From what I can see, Moon One is a perfect twin to the moon I watched with Mum every night before she died.

But Moon Two has a strange blue-gray tint, and as I look through the telescope, I feel like I'm exploring a whole new world. Dad points out the Ocean of Uncertainty, where he tells me Yuri Gagarin touched down in the Lunar 3 lander. He shows me the Sea of Honey ringed by the Heisenberg Mountains and, in the middle of this, the huge Everett crater looking down on us like a giant eye. On this second moon everything seems different, the unfamiliar shadows giving the man in the moon a strange new face.

Drinking mugs of cocoa that Dad's warmed up on the camping stove, we sit on the patio steps together beneath the two moons. With Dad sitting next to me, I feel like I'm finally home, but whenever I look up into the sky, I see a massive reminder that this isn't my world.

"You know," Dad says, sipping from his mug, "I bet your mum would've solved this energy crisis by now. She was always coming up with brilliant ideas. When you were a baby, we used to take you out for walks on the moors to get you to go to sleep, and while we were walking we'd chat about what we could do if the coal ever ran out. You'd be there in your buggy, your little toy windmill turning madly in the breeze, and your mum and I used to think up all these crazy schemes.

"Once I had the idea of building a chain of windmills stretching across the moor. I thought we could use the power of the wind to provide the energy that Clackthorpe would need to make its own electricity. I know it sounds like wishful thinking, but your mum thought it just might work."

Dad drains his cocoa and then lets out a weary sigh. "But then she got ill, and there wasn't any time for us to chase after such stupid dreams."

I look up at Dad, the twin moons illuminating the sadness in his eyes as he stares up into the darkness. In another world he's a scientist. In another universe he's saved the world. And now he has the chance to do the same here.

"Why don't we try to make it now?" I ask.

Dad stares back at me in surprise, then laughs out loud. In his eyes I see the same look the Dad in my universe has whenever he tries one of his crazy experiments on his TV show.

"OK," he says with a grin. "Let's do it."

With candles and lanterns lighting up the workshop, we set to work. Dad's taken the alternator out of Granddad Joe's old Ford Ka, and it's now sitting on the workbench waiting to be transformed into the generator for the wind turbine. I'm busy removing the back wheel and gears from "my" bike and hoping that the Albie in this universe won't mind when he finds out.

On the workbench, Dad's screwing together the wind-mill blades that he's made out of the venetian blinds that were hanging in the kitchen. He's cut these down to size, twisting and then screwing the slats together to give each blade extra strength. As he finishes the last one, he steps over to help me pull the back wheel of the bike free, lifting it up onto the workbench, ready to fix the windmill blades into place.

"So you really think this is going to work?" he asks me.

I nod excitedly as Dad starts to bolt each of the blades to the back wheel.

"It's the energy of the future," I tell him, thinking of the wind turbines I see stretching across the moors in my universe. "And the best thing is, it'll never run out."

The clock on the wall of the shed says it's almost midnight. I don't think I've slept for nearly twenty-four hours, and in that time I've traveled to three parallel universes, met different versions of myself, stolen an animatronic platypus, and busted out some old-school hip-hop moves. But the funny thing is, as Dad and I work together to fit the wind turbine's pulleys and gears into place, I don't feel tired at all.

All I've ever wanted is for Dad to stop racing around the world and spend some time with me. Not a part-time dad, but a proper dad who's there when I need him. A dad who listens to what I say, just like Mum did. Now, in this world that has two moons shining down outside, I've finally got what I want.

I look up at the top of the shed where Dad has attached our homemade wind turbine. The windmill blades and bicycle wheel are silhouetted by the blue-gray globe of Moon Two as it slowly starts to set.

"Ready?" Dad asks.

I nod as he reaches up to flick a switch. As the windmill blades turn and the bike wheel spins, the fairy lights we've hung everywhere suddenly light up the garden, instantly turning night into day.

"It works," Dad says, shaking his head in wonder. "Your mum always said it would. With enough of these wind turbine things, we could generate enough electricity to power the whole village. Maybe even the whole world." He turns toward me with a grin. "We did it, Albie!"

Suddenly I feel incredibly tired. I want to tell Dad how happy I am, but all that comes out when I open my mouth is a massive yawn.

"Come on," Dad says, putting his arm around my shoulder. "That's enough saving the world for one night. Let's get you to bed."

In the corner of the attic room, I can see my cardboard box tucked under the eaves, the quantum banana experiment hidden safely inside.

I sit down on the edge of the bed, barely able to keep my eyes open.

"Straight to sleep now, Albie," Dad says, standing in the doorway. "We'll have plenty of time to work out what to do with our invention tomorrow. Maybe we can go down to London and show it to the government scientists who are working on the energy crisis. Let them know we've found a possible solution at last."

"That sounds great, Dad," I tell him, fighting back another yawn. "It's been a brilliant day."

Dad smiles.

"Your mum was right," he says. "When we stick together, we can do anything."

Then he quietly closes the bedroom door, leaving me alone in the dark.

I sit there for a second, staring up at the twin moons through the skylight. I know the Albie in this universe is due back from his school trip tomorrow. I should get off the bed and climb inside my cardboard box. But I'm just too tired, and I can't stop myself from lying down. I just need to rest my eyes for a minute. . . .

"Dad, I'm home!"

The sound of my own voice coming up the stairs wakes me up out of the deepest sleep I've ever known. For a second I don't know where I am. Then I see the poster of the solar system hanging above my bed—two moons in orbit around the planet Earth.

Now I remember. This isn't my bedroom. This isn't even my universe.

Dad's voice floats up the stairs in reply.

"Albie," he says, and I can hear the surprise in his voice from here. "I didn't expect to see you up so early after we had such a late night. I've just been out in the garden to check on the wind turbine. It's still working."

"The wind what?"

I jump off the bed, scrambling toward the cardboard box that's tucked under the eaves. I can't stay here any longer. That's not my dad downstairs. I've only had him on loan.

I climb inside the box, pulling my knees up to my chest to fit inside, and close the flaps behind me. In the corner, Mum's laptop is still working away silently, a blur of zeroes and ones scrolling across the screen. A handful of feathers are scattered across the keyboard, and I quickly check that the Geiger counter and quantum entangler are still connected as I hear the sound of footsteps coming up the stairs.

I grab hold of the banana, feeling it squish beneath my fingers. In the supermarket they give bananas a best-before date, but what I need to know now is its radioactive half-life. As soon as a single atom inside this banana decays, then the Geiger counter will click and get me out of this place.

In every parallel universe I've found so far, Mum's still been gone. I don't think I'll ever be able to find her again. But then I remember what Dad said to me yesterday.

"When your mum died, I felt lost. But you helped me face up to things, Albie. You made me see that life was still worth living."

Dad's still lost in my own universe, but now I know he needs me too.

I hold the banana next to the Geiger counter, praying that this time it'll take me home.

CLICK.

Then the universe shivers and the box goes dark.

I'M TOO SCARED AT FIRST TO OPEN THE BOX, frightened at what I might find when I look outside. Stalling, I pick up Alba's quantum entangler, unscrewing the lid of the thermos and tipping out the ammonite necklace into the palm of my hand. It was a great plan, I think to myself. Just a shame it didn't work.

I take a deep breath and then push open the flaps on top of the box. Everything is dark. The Quantum Banana Theory must have done its new trick of skipping from day to night in this switch to a brand-new universe. But as I climb out of the box and look around the room, I realize that it hasn't taken me home.

This isn't my bedroom. The skylight's in the same place,

but there's no telescope, no piles of books and comics on the floor. Then, as my eyes adjust to the gloom, I see something on the wall that makes me stop and stare.

It's Paddington Bear in his red hat and blue duffel coat. He's sitting on a suitcase eating a marmalade sandwich. In fact, there are dozens of Paddington Bears all over the wall. This is the wallpaper I had in my nursery when I was a baby, and as I turn around, I see a white cot standing where my bed should be.

I stand there frozen for a second—my brain flashing up error messages as I try to make sense of this. Then I hear the sound of footsteps coming up the stairs, before the door is pushed open and somebody steps into the bedroom.

"If it's that cat again . . ."

It's my mum.

I can see her framed in the light spilling in from the landing, her long, dark hair just the same as it was before she got ill. Mum peers toward the shadows where I'm standing.

"Who's there?"

For a second I stay frozen, unable to believe that I've found her at last. Then I step forward out of the shadows.

"It's me—Albie."

Mum stares at me with a look of total confusion on her face. She puts her hand on her stomach, and when I look down at the bump there, I realize she's pregnant. Then

Mum's knees start to buckle, and I rush forward to stop her from falling down.

"You can't be . . . ," she murmurs as I help her into the easy chair next to the door. Around her neck Mum's wearing the ammonite necklace, the spiral fossil gleaming gold in the half-light. "It's impossible."

I shake my head in reply.

"You only find out what's possible by trying to do the impossible. That's what you told me, Mum."

I open my hand to show her what I'm holding. In my palm, the spiral ammonite on its chain gleams gold. A mirror image of the fossil on the chain around her neck.

Mum stares at it in disbelief. Then she looks up at me with wonder in her eyes.

"It *is* you," she whispers, reaching out to touch my face. "I could never forget your eyes."

A tear rolls down Mum's cheek, and I can't quite work out why she's sad. I've found her at last.

"But how?" she says, the words coming out in a silent sigh.

So I tell her everything. How she died and how Dad told me that quantum physics said there was another universe where she was still alive. How I invented the Quantum Banana Theory to find her again, kidnapping my next-door neighbor's cat and traveling to parallel worlds. I tell her about my evil twin and how I had to steal a duck-billed platypus. I tell her about Alba and the accident and how

Alba wanted me to let Mum know that she loves her. I tell her that my dad is lost without her—just like me.

And she listens to me, holding my hand in hers, just like she always did.

"So where's all my stuff?" I ask her when I finally run out of breath, looking around the room. "Are you booting me out for the new baby?"

Mum looks at me with tears in her eyes.

"This is your room," she says, her voice cracking a little. "You died when you were just a baby, Albie. The doctors did everything they could, but your heart just wasn't strong enough."

I'm holding on to Mum's hand, but I feel like I'm falling into a black hole. Dad's book said that a parallel universe might have one tiny change, and in this universe it's me.

"It hit me and your dad very hard," Mum says, wiping away a tear. "For years we kept your nursery just like it is now. We couldn't even think of trying for another baby. I only got to hold you for a little while, but I didn't think I'd ever feel the same way again. Then this year we found out that I'm pregnant. The scan says it's going to be a little girl."

I'm biting my bottom lip so hard it almost bleeds, but I can't stop myself from crying.

I don't know if I'm crying for the baby Albie, who never got the chance to grow up, or the baby sister I'll never even know. For Alba, for Granddad Joe, even for my evil twin, but most of all for my mum.

And Mum holds me as I cry, stroking my hair and telling me that she's here.

I look up at her kind face, just the same as I remember it. There's still one question I need to ask.

"Do you believe in heaven?"

Mum cradles my head so I'm looking up at the skylight. I can see the stars shining there, tiny points of white against the blackness of the night.

"Hundreds of years ago, they used to call the sky the heavens," she tells me, the sound of her voice a warm, cozy blanket that I just want to snuggle down in. "The sun and the moon and all the thousands of stars they could see. Now we know that in our galaxy alone—the Milky Way— there are a hundred billion stars. And there are a hundred billion galaxies across the universe. Thousands of new stars are being born every second, and thousands are dying too. And when these stars explode in a supernova, they scatter the elements that make everything—hydrogen, helium, oxygen, and everything else—across the universe to make new stars and planets and, in the end, us." Mum looks down at me with a gentle smile on her face. "There's a piece of heaven inside you, and there's a piece of heaven inside me. We're all made of stardust." Then she hugs me, whispering in my ear as she holds me tight. "I know there's a heaven, Albie, because it's given me the chance to see you again."

I hold on to my mum as tightly as I can. I never want this hug to end, but it has to.

Everything I've done was because I couldn't imagine the world without my mum, but now I know there's someone else who needs me too.

"I've got to go," I say, wiping my eyes as I get to my feet. "I've got to get back for Dad."

Mum slowly nods, her eyes still shining with tears.

"Goodbye, Albie," she says. "I love you."

"I love you too, Mum. I always will."

Then I turn away and don't look back as I crawl inside the cardboard box. If I turn around, I don't think I'll ever be able to go. Closing the lid behind me, I hunch down in the bottom, my shoulders shaking as I try to stop myself from crying my heart out. Then Dylan jumps onto my lap.

At first I think he's going to claw me, but instead he just purrs and I hold him tight as the laptop screen fills with a blur of numbers. I don't even know if the Quantum Banana Theory can take us home. Dad said there could be an infinite number of parallel universes, but Dylan seems to think I know the way back.

"We've just got to wait for a particle to decay," I whisper in his ear, his fur warm and sticky against my face. "Then we'll see where we end up this time."

And that's when Dylan decides to eat the banana.

As soon as he takes a bite, Dylan starts to make a really

weird noise like he's coughing up a hairball backward. His claws dig into my legs and his meow now sounds like a death rattle. I'm trapped inside a box with a psychopathic cat, and it looks like he's turning zombie on me.

Dad's book said that when a radioactive particle decays, the universe splits in two. But the book also said that if anything interferes with the particle, this creates "quantum decoherence" and the universe collapses into a single state. And with the radioactive particle inside the banana now in Dylan's stomach, I reckon this counts as pretty *major* interference. The only question is: will Dylan's midnight feast zap us back to our own universe, or send us spiraling into a black hole?

Then Dylan throws up the banana, peel and all, all over the Geiger counter.

As he slowly unclenches his claws, I notice through a crack in the lid of the box that it's light outside. It's gone from night to day again. The universe must have changed without me even noticing.

I don't know what I'm going to find outside, but Dylan isn't hanging around to worry about that. He pushes the cardboard flaps open with his nose and shoots out of the box like a cat out of hell.

"What's that?"

I peek out of the box to see my dad standing in the doorway of my bedroom, looking down in surprise as Dylan races between his legs and straight down the stairs.

I look around the room carefully, making sure that this time I've found the right universe. Everything seems to be there—my telescope, my books, my comics—and as I look at the poster of the solar system above my bed, all the planets are in the right place with the right number of moons. It looks like I'm home.

When Dylan took a bite out of the banana, he must have short-circuited the experiment. The Quantum Banana Theory got a factory reset, restoring us to our original universe. I let out a sigh of relief. I owe that cat another LolCat treat.

Dad looks at me quizzically as I climb out of the cardboard box.

"Your granddad said you'd come home early from school."

I nod, waiting for the lecture to start about how we should all be getting back to normal.

"Me too," he says, and then I see his eyes fill with tears as he wraps his arms around me. I'm crying too now, but through my sobs I can hear Dad telling me that we're going to be OK.

Despite what the book the vicar gave me said about five stages of grief, I don't think there's a set of rules you follow when you lose someone you love. All you can do is hope you'll find a way through.

Dad pulls a tissue out of his pocket and pushes it into my hand.

"Seeing as we've both finished early," he says, his arm still holding me tight as I wipe my tears away, "how about we do something together instead?"

Mum's gone, but Dad's still here and we've got to go on living. That's what Mum wanted. And that's what we're going to do.

THE SCHOOL HALL IS PACKED FOR THE SCIENCE
fair. All the tables are set up in rows like it's exam time, but
instead of boring tests, each one is displaying a different
science project. There's Olivia Appleby's potato-powered
clock, Michael Bedford's robot racers, and Meera Patel's
dry-ice bubble maker, Meera poking each giant bubble
with a knitting needle and making them pop in a shower
of smoke.

All the mums and dads from Class 6 are wander-
ing around the aisles, looking proud as they inspect the
experiments. There's a small crowd gathered at Victoria
Barnes's table as she shows off her working model of Mount
Vesuvius. Pouring in a bottle of vinegar, Victoria steps back
theatrically as an eruption of lava foams out of the crater

at the top. The orange-red gloop spills down the sides of her papier-mâché volcano, wiping out the Lego town of Pompeii and covering the toy soldiers and plastic farm animals in a layer of pretend lava. Everyone claps and Victoria looks dead smug, like she's got first prize in the bag.

But Miss Benjamin is already starting to shepherd everyone outside, following Kiran, Dad, and me as we carry the huge balloon through the double doors and out into the playground. As I walk past Wesley MacNamara's table, he gives me a friendly grin. Wesley's standing in front of a poster that reads "DUCK-BILLED PLATYPUS—ALIEN OR NOT?" In a glass case on his table is the stuffed platypus that Dad convinced the Clackthorpe Museum of Natural History and Mechanical Wonders to lend to the school for the science fair. I don't think I have to worry about getting a dead arm anymore.

The rest of the school is waiting outside in the playground, every class lined up with their teacher to see the science fair's grand finale. Everyone's excited to see the celebrity from TV—otherwise known as my dad—although some of the little ones from Early Years look a bit disappointed that he's not from the kids' channel.

Following Dad's advice, Kiran dropped the idea of sending his My Little Pony balloons into space, and instead we're using a high-altitude weather balloon that Dad borrowed from his TV show. Fixed to the bottom of this is

Alba's quantum entangler, and inside that I've put Mum's ashes.

"I'm sorry these aren't going to be the first ashes sent into space," I tell Kiran as we reach the middle of the playground. "That guy from *Star Trek* got there first."

Kiran shakes his head as we look up into the clear blue sky.

"Your mum's going to be the first Nobel Prize winner in space," he says. "She was a scientific genius. That's what they said on the TV."

Since I used Mum's laptop in the quantum banana experiment, all its data got sent back to CERN via the Grid. When the scientists there looked at what Mum's data said, they all got very excited. They say the data she found might actually prove that parallel universes exist. It's never happened before, but some people are saying Mum might even be given the Nobel Prize in Physics, even though she's passed away.

Dad puts his hand on my shoulder as I hold on to the balloon. I can feel the helium inside tugging on my wrist, pulling my arm toward the sky.

"Ready?" he asks.

Most of the time you need to hold on tight to the things you love. It's just like flying a kite. But sometimes you realize that you need to let them go.

Looking up at my dad, I nod. Then I open my hand.

Everyone cheers as the balloon shoots up into the sky. Shielding my eyes, I watch it rise. It's the size of a beach ball now, getting smaller with every second. Beneath the balloon I can still just see the quantum entangler glinting in the sunlight. The altimeter fixed to it will automatically open the lid when it hits the edge of space, scattering Mum's ashes.

We're all made of stardust. And when I look up at the sky at night—into the heavens—Mum will always be there.

The Science of
The MANY WORLDS of ALBIE BRIGHT

From radioactive bananas to cats that are both dead and alive at the same time, here's more about the real-life science in *The Many Worlds of Albie Bright*.

Wait a minute, are bananas really radioactive?
Here's the info: A single banana contains at least 0.1 microsievert of radiation. That's about the same amount of radiation you'd be exposed to if you lived next door to a nuclear power plant for a year. But don't worry, this level of radiation isn't harmful to you. In fact, if your dentist gives you an X-ray, you're actually exposed to 10 microsieverts of radiation. That's one hundred times the dose you'd get from a single banana.

But what about Schrödinger's cat? Did that crazy scientist really try to poison poor Tiddles?
Sadly, we don't know if Erwin Schrödinger had a pet cat called Tiddles. His famous experiment is actually a *thought* experiment—a way of imagining the weird world of quantum physics.

What exactly is quantum physics?
Until the end of the nineteenth century, scientists thought

that atoms—the tiny particles that make up all matter—were the smallest things that existed, but then they discovered that atoms were made of *even smaller particles* called protons, neutrons, and electrons. Quantum physics is the theory that scientists have developed to describe and explain how these subatomic particles behave.

Like a single atom being in more than one place at the same time?
Exactly! When Albie's dad tells him about the double-slit experiment, he's describing an actual experiment that scientists can perform in real life. If they repeatedly fire electrons at a detector plate with two slits set in front of it, scientists discover something very strange. Over time, a pattern builds up on the detector plate—a pattern that could be produced only if waves of electrons were interfering with each other. This should be impossible, because the scientists only fire a single electron at a time.

And in 1926, Erwin Schrödinger came up with an equation to explain this "*waveform.*"

An equation for *what*?
Schrödinger's equation describes how the electron exists as a wave of probability. This means the electron is spread throughout space, all at once, but there is a higher probability of finding it in some places than others. Some scientists say the "interference pattern" on the detector

plate is produced by the electron taking *every* possible path to the detection plate—at the same time!

But . . . but . . . but—that's crazy!
Wait a second, it gets even weirder! If a scientist tries to track the path of the electron, the interference pattern disappears and the electron acts like a particle—not a wave—going through either the left- or right-hand slit. To explain this, a Danish physicist named Niels Bohr came up with a theory that became known as the Copenhagen Interpretation.

The Copenhagen Interpretation—that sounds like the title of a cool sci-fi film!
It's a sci-fi theory, too! The Copenhagen Interpretation says that watching the electron causes the wave of probabilities to collapse into a definite position. But until you take a look, all the different possibilities exist at the same time.

That's even crazier! How can an electron know that someone's watching it?
That's what Schrödinger thought. Writing to his friend Albert Einstein, Schrödinger came up with his "cat in the box" thought experiment to prove how crazy the Copenhagen Interpretation was. As Albie's dad explains in his book:

A cat is put inside a box with a lump of radioactive uranium that has a 50 percent chance of decaying. This means that at any moment, there is a 50 percent chance of a radioactive particle being emitted. If the Geiger counter detects a radioactive particle, it will trigger the hammer and smash open the bottle of poison. This will kill the cat. However, quantum physics says that until the box is opened and we take a look, the particle will be in both possible states—decayed and undecayed—simultaneously. This means the cat inside the box is dead and alive at the same time!

In the real world, there's no way something can be dead AND alive at the same time. However, scientists working in a laboratory HAVE managed to film atoms existing in two different states at the same time—just like Schrödinger's cat!

Okay, so bananas are radioactive, and an atom can be in two different places at once, but parallel universes don't exist—do they?
We just don't know. According to Hugh Everett's Many-Worlds Interpretation of quantum physics, our universe is constantly splitting into new parallel universes. In his theory, taking a look at the electron being fired in the double-slit experiment doesn't just cause the wave of

probable places the electron could be to collapse into one, it causes the universe to split into different universes for every probable position the electron could be in! In one universe, a scientist will see the electron go through the left-hand slit, and in another universe, a different version of the same scientist will see the electron go through the right-hand slit! As Albie's dad explains, "Everything that can happen *does* happen somewhere."

So can I jump into a cardboard box like Albie to travel to these parallel worlds and meet a different version of me?

Not so fast! Albie's cardboard box came with a quantum computer that was hooked up to the Large Hadron Collider at Cern, near Geneva, Switzerland. So far in the real world, scientists have only been able to build simple quantum computers to solve single problems, so you won't be able to use one to help you to hop to a parallel world—yet! However, the atom-smashing experiments that scientists are performing at the Large Hadron Collider might be able to detect mini black holes that could provide evidence for the existence of different dimensions where these parallel universes hide. So maybe one day we'll be able to find many worlds filled with copies of you and me, just like Albie did. . . .

ABOUT THE AUTHOR

Christopher Edge grew up in Manchester, England, where he spent most of his childhood in the local library dreaming up stories, but now lives in Gloucestershire, where he spends most of his time in the local library dreaming up stories. Before becoming a writer, he worked as an English teacher, an editor, and a publisher—any job that let him keep a book close at hand. When not writing, he also works as a freelance publisher and education consultant, encouraging children to read. Visit Christopher at christopheredge.co.uk and follow him online.